THE WEANING

HANNAH studied Drama & English at UEA and gained her MA in Creative & Critical Writing at Kingston University. Her first novel *Alarm Girl* is published by Myriad.

THE WEANING

HANNAH VINCENT

LONDON

PUBLISHED BY SALT PUBLISHING 2018

2 4 6 8 10 9 7 5 3 1

First published in Great Britain in 2018 by
Salt Publishing Ltd
International House, 24 Holborn Viaduct, London EC1A 2BN United Kingdom

www.saltpublishing.com

Salt Publishing Limited Reg. No. 5293401

A CIP catalogue record for this book is available from the British Library

ISBN 978 1 78463 120 8 (Paperback edition)
ISBN 978 1 78463 121 5 (Electronic edition)

Typeset in Neacademia by Salt Publishing

Printed and bound in Great Britain by Clays Ltd, St Ives plc

Salt Publishing Limited is committed to responsible forest management.
This book is made from Forest Stewardship Council™ certified paper.

To Fox and cubs

§

THE BRASS DOORKNOCKER is shaped like a hand. I take the hand in mine and knock.

I have an interview with 'Nikki' who needs a childminder. My First Aid training and child safety certificates are in my bag.

No answer. I knock again then check my phone to make sure I have the right house.

M sleeping so pls don't knock – ring when u get here thanx

From somewhere inside, a door bangs and footsteps sound. A woman opens the door. Her dark hair is cut into a neat, geometric style and contrasts with her white linen dress. She wears Kohl eye make-up, silver bangles and a plain silver necklace.

'I'm Bobbi,' I say. 'Sorry, I didn't get your text till after I knocked. Did I wake him?'

She tells me it's alright, the baby's still asleep and to come on in. I wipe my feet on the doormat, which has the word 'Enter' written on it in black letters.

'Take them off if you like,' Nikki says.

'Shall I?'

She has bare feet.

'If you like – whatever makes you feel comfortable.'

She waits while I take off my shoes. I remove my socks too and stuff them inside my bag alongside my certificates.

'Come through, we're in the garden.'

I am barefoot like her. The black and white tiles of the hallway feel cool. She ushers me down a corridor lined with framed black and white photographs on the walls. One of the photographs shows an exotic looking beach, another is of a wedding and there is a large close-up portrait of a baby. Nikki pauses at the end of the hallway while I study the portrait.

'That's him,' she says.

'He's beautiful.'

'He's going to be a heartbreaker, that's for sure.'

The baby looks at me with a serious expression. He has the dark hair and dark eyes of an Indian prince or a 1940s cinema idol. I hold his stare while his mother waits.

At the end of the hallway, double doors lead onto a pretty walled garden. Toys are laid out on a rug and a woman sits at a patio table, eyes closed, her face lifted to the sun.

'My health visitor,' Nikki explains.

'I'm just going,' the health visitor says, but she doesn't move.

Nikki's bracelets jangle as she pours me some water from a jug.

'That's pretty,' she says, noticing the tattoo on my wrist of a Russian doll, cheerful and rosy-cheeked. I hold out my wrist and Babushka smiles at us.

'It must have hurt,' the health visitor says. 'Having it done there where the skin's so thin.'

Her eyes are still closed so I don't know how she has seen my tattoo.

I get my certificates out of my bag. One of my socks tumbles onto the wrought iron table and I quickly pocket it. An electronic baby monitor in the middle of the table crackles and lets out a sigh.

'We'll go and get him in a bit,' Nikki says.

But this baby is eager to meet me – the monitor lets out a yelp and the lights on its display bounce. The health visitor opens her eyes at last and scrapes her chair away from the table.

'I'll leave you to it,' she says.

We follow her to the front door where she reminds Nikki of their next appointment. Nikki writes the date in a thick desk diary on the hallway table. Once the health visitor has left, Nikki turns to me.

'I'm struggling, to be honest,' she says. 'I'm just not confident I know what I'm doing.'

'I'm sure you're doing everything fine,' I tell her.

'One of the reasons I thought you might be suitable,' she says, 'is that you're a bit older and a mother yourself.'

She lays her pen down on the open diary. 'Is it a girl or a boy you've got?'

'One of each.'

'Nice. That's what I want.'

We climb the stairs and outside a closed door on the uppermost landing Nikki holds a finger to her lips. She opens the door and we move into the room. I can hear the baby breathing. He stirs. Soft carpet presses between my toes. Nikki opens the curtains a chink and a bar of sunlight reveals him lying in a cot in the centre of the room. He turns his head to follow his mother. In the womb he would have been sensitive to shifts from dark to light, from asleep to awake, and now here he is, outside of her body, waiting to see what will happen.

'I like him to have a gentle waking rhythm,' Nikki whispers.

The baby lies still, trying to decipher the sounds his mother is making. I take a step closer and he hears me, turns his face. His dark eyes hold mine and the rest of the world falls away. I have never met this child but I know him. I know him, and I feel sure he knows me – the intelligence in his eyes tell me so.

'Hello, Pickle' Nikki says. 'Hello, Babu.'

She lifts him out of his cot, carrying him to the window where she opens the curtains fully. He blinks in the sunshine, twisting in her arms to look at me.

'Who's this, Marcel? Who's this, eh?'

She bounces him on her hip.

'Hello, Marcel,' I say, and I take his hand to save me from drowning in the dark of his eyes.

'I'll show you around,' Nikki says. 'Come.'

Still holding her child's small warm hand, I follow her out of the room. On the landing, his mother opens another door.

'Guest room.'

We stand on the threshold, poking our faces into the room, which has sloping eaves and a tiny fireplace, like a doll's house.

'I guess if we have another baby this will be his or hers,' says Nikki.

'Are you planning to have another one?'

'Oh yes, but not for a year or so – give this little monkey some time of his own first.'

His fingers are tight around two of mine as we move downstairs to the second floor. His dark head bobs against Nikki's white linen shoulder.

'Our room,' she says, holding open a door.

A smell of lavender hangs in the air and there are more black and white photographs like the ones downstairs, including a framed contact sheet on the wall above the marital bed which charts the pregnancy of a faceless, naked woman.

'My husband took those,' Nikki says, following my gaze.

'Is he a photographer?'

'Writer. You'll meet him.'

'What kind of things does he write?'

'Oh, it's ghost-writing projects mainly – that's where the money is. But there have been a couple of novels.'

She rearranges some necklaces that lie on the top of a chest of drawers. Marcel watches her movements and lets go of my hand to reach for the jewellery.

'Not those,' she says. 'They're mummy's.'

'And what is it that you do?' I ask.

'I'm a PR officer for a charity campaigning to raise awareness of modern-day slaves,' she says.

'Are there still slaves, then?' I ask.

'You'd be surprised. And not just overseas. There have been prosecutions in this country.'

She turns and leads the way across the landing to a white-tiled bathroom. The window is open and looks out into the tops of trees. Their fresh green smell fills the space and mingles with the perfume of expensive soap – sandalwood and cinnamon. A white painted washstand holds a changing mat printed with yellow ducklings.

'He's in washable nappies,' Nikki says. 'Trying to do our bit.'

She opens an airing cupboard that is neatly stacked with nappies, flannels and towels. All three of us stare at the clean linens. Then she wrinkles her nose and sniffs.

'Have you done something?'

'Sorry?'

'Not you. He's terribly constipated – just the tiniest nuggets but no real issue. Would you mind? It's a two-man job.'

She lays Marcel on the duckling changing mat and asks me to hold down his arms. He stares at me as his mother pulls off his clothes and inspects the contents of his nappy. I smile at him, but he remains solemn.

'Poor lamb, you really are bunged up, aren't you,' Nikki says.

She holds both his ankles, lifting them in one hand to clean his bottom with the other, wiping, then releasing his ankles and dabbing quickly at his penis with a fresh wipe. Then she fastens a new nappy and asks if I will take him. My fingertips scrape against the cool plastic of the changing mat as I pick him up and I can't help rocking from one foot to another – as if his weight sets off a rhythm inside me. I kiss his hair. He smells of warm bed.

'I can see you two are going to get along,' Nikki says, glancing at us in the mirror above the sink where she is washing her hands. Then she turns to face me.

'I don't suppose you could spare an hour or two now, could you? I could get some work done while you hang out in the garden.'

'Of course,' I say.

'Wonderful! Thank you so much!'

We go downstairs with me treading oh so carefully, imagining how his little body would thud and bounce if I dropped him.

'Lounge.'

This room is large and airy, furnished with leather sofas, Indian rugs, and an old-fashioned writing desk in one corner. The walls are hung with large abstract paintings.

'Who's the artist?' I ask.

'My father-in-law,' Nikki says. 'He was quite famous in his day. I'm not sure I like his work much, but there you have it.'

She gazes at the canvases and so does Marcel. He has the poise of a miniature Maharajah surveying his estate, but I feel him tense with excitement when Nikki pulls out a crate from the bottom shelf of a bookcase.

'Toys.'

She shoves the crate back into place and our tour of the house ends in the basement kitchen where I am shown bottles and teats in a state-of-the-art steriliser.

'He usually has a bottle around now,' she says. 'Would you like me to feed him?'

'You're sure you don't mind?'

'Of course not.'

'And this would be gratis?'

'Sorry?'

'A free trial, as it were.'

She fixes me with her brown-black eyes.

'Yes,' I say.

She makes up a bottle and watches me settle with her child on one of the dining chairs, which are transparent, made from clear Perspex or fibre glass.

'Give me a shout if you need anything,' she says.

'We won't need anything,' I say.

Marcel watches her go out of the room as I tilt the bottle to his mouth. The gesture, the angle, everything about this movement is as familiar as if I were tilting it to mine. He begins to suck but keeps his gaze fixed on the space his mother has left. When he realises she isn't coming back he turns his eyes on me, staring into my face. I pretend not to notice his interest, looking around the room to allow him to study me while he feeds.

The kitchen cabinets and surfaces are white and everything gleams. The black and white floor tiles are like a giant chessboard. An old-fashioned clock hangs on one wall, while on the other a poster shows a friendly nurse in a starched white head-dress. She holds a tray on which there is a packet bearing the same image, of the benign-looking nurse with rosebud lips and shiny cheeks, holding her tray which carries the same packet with the same image, and so on into infinity, it seems. I stare and stare at the poster, trying to locate the tiniest nurse, losing myself in her labyrinth, while Marcel's head, with its dark, soft hair, weighs against my arm. We are mother and child. The fibre glass of the chair, the plastic of the bottle, the metal of the microwave, kettle, toaster - these things are manufactured while this baby and I, we are flesh, we are Nature. I close my eyes. The clock sounds its soft, steady tick and Marcel sucks to the same rhythm. A bird is singing and I can hear train announcements coming from the nearby railway station.

When he has finished his milk, Marcel pops the teat out of his mouth and straightens his little legs, straining his body forwards, trying to sit upright.

'Shall we go in the garden?' I ask him.

We rinse his bottle at the sink, then go outside where the air is warm after the cool basement. I lay Marcel down and he bats my hair, which I swish to and fro in front of him. He manages to catch a fistful and when I loosen his fingers there are a few strands left in his grip. I sprinkle these onto the grass for some bird to collect for its nest. After hair swishing, we lie side by side looking up into the branches of an overhanging tree, the coolness of the ground seeping through the rug. He doesn't have the strength yet to roll onto his front, so I push his little body, showing him how it will feel when he can do it for himself. I roll him over and then back again, and then, because I like the weight of him against my hand; the resistance of his little body as it tips from one position to another, I do it again and again until he complains. Then I hold him upright and he paddles his little feet in my lap, marching on the spot to my rendition of 'The Grand Old Duke of York'.

Some time later, Nikki sticks her head out of an upstairs window.

'It's time for his lunch,' she calls, ' but can you give me five more minutes? I'm waiting for an ebay bid'

I give her a thumbs-up and wave Marcel's hand in reply, but she has already disappeared.

'Have you had a lovely time?' she asks when she joins us.

She holds out her arms for Marcel and kisses him loudly when I pass him to her. We return indoors where she fastens a plastic bib around his neck and straps him into a high chair. She takes an ice-cube tray out of the freezer.

'For his lunch, just pop one of these into a bowl and zap it for thirty seconds,' she says.

All three of us wait for the microwave timer to ping.

When it is ready, she stirs the food and makes approving noises. But Marcel doesn't want the purée. He turns his face away and when she tries again he cries out and thrashes his body from side to side to avoid the spoon.

'Everything's a battle,' Nikki says.

'Shall I have a go?' I ask.

Nikki hands me the dish and I touch the spoon to my own lips.

'I'd prefer it if you didn't do that,' she says, fetching a replacement from a drawer.

She watches me dip the clean spoon into the food and hold it out. Marcel arches his body away from me.

'This isn't working,' Nikki says, getting him out of the high chair.

'He's probably not that hungry,' I say. 'He drank a bottle fairly recently, after all.'

The baby flails in his mother's arms, crying now. I try to catch his hand and soothe him by singing some of the songs he enjoyed in the garden, but he is wailing and can't hear me.

My time is up. Nikki leads me to the front door with Marcel complaining in her arms. She jiggles him up and down, shushing him while I sit on the stairs to put my shoes and socks back on.

'Sometimes I wonder if it would be different if he was a girl,' she says.

She opens the door and Marcel grows calmer. Nikki plucks a leaf from a bay tree that stands on the top step, holding the leaf under her nose before allowing it to flutter to the ground.

'Thank you for your time,' she says. 'How would you feel about working for us?'

'That would be wonderful,' I say.

A tear trembles in Marcel's eyelashes. I lean forward to kiss him goodbye, but Nikki is surprised by my gesture and steps backwards on to the 'Enter' door mat, stumbling slightly. To cover up any awkwardness I kiss her too.

'I'll be in touch,' she says.

A smell of dust rises off the pavement and the sky darkens behind the tall white houses. By the time I am halfway down the hill, big spots of rain hit the pavement and there is a rumble of thunder. A bus slows to a halt, its brakes whining, and as I hop on there is a loud crack and a torrential burst of rain.

'Just in time!' I say, but the driver doesn't respond other than to scoop the coins I place in the tray and hand me a ticket. Other passengers lift their heads from phones and newspapers to stare out of the spattered windows. Our breath mists the glass.

The bus winds down the hill and through town. A young woman gets on and sits in the seat in front of me. She holds her phone in front of her face and I can see from the postage-stamp-sized image in the right hand corner of the screen who she is talking to: a man and a woman walking through a city at night. They must be in a different time zone. They aren't speaking English. From the way they smile at the girl, I assume she is their daughter. They are pleased to hear from her, they are delighted she rang, they want to know how she is doing in a country far, far away from where they are. The girl chatters without noticing me watching over her shoulder. I am part of her conversation with her parents, even though I can't understand anything they are saying. I will go and see my mother tomorrow.

I am so engrossed in the foreign girl's conversation with her parents I almost miss my stop. It's raining hard so I duck inside the mini market at the end of our road. The bell on the shop door rings as I slam it behind me. Sameer, the shopkeeper, looks up from his task. He is re-stocking the cigarette display behind his counter. Smoking Kills.

What to make for tea? I pick up a box of eggs. My kids will complain, but an omelette is cheap and quick. I add a chocolate bar and a packet of bubble gum as compensation, and place the items on the counter among Sameer's jumble of cigarette packets. Protect Children: don't let them breathe your smoke.

The bell rings again and we both look round to see a man with silver hair wiping his feet on the mat just inside the shop doorway. It is my new neighbour, shaking himself like a dog. He moved into my street only a couple of months ago and I have watched him renovate his house, sanding and painting the front door, carrying building materials in and out, working by himself. I thought he might have a family who would move in with him once the house was finished, but he seems to be living there by himself.

'Alright?' he says, nodding at Sameer and me.

He grabs an onion from the vegetable rack, tosses it in the air and catches it. Sameer continues to slot packets of cigarettes onto the shelves behind his counter while I dig in my bag for my purse.

'Taking up smoking?' asks my neighbour.

He gestures at the jumble of cigarette packets on the counter.

'Always,' I say.

His eyes are very blue. He gives Sameer the exact money for his onion. His hands are freckled with paint. Warning: Smoking is highly addictive: Don't start. I pay for my shopping and, pocketing the sweets I have bought, I move to the door.

'Ready to make a run for it?' my neighbour says.

He holds out his jacket above both our heads.

'It's only water,' I say.

I step out of the shop.

'You're right,' he says, lowering his jacket.

Rain plasters our hair to our faces.

'Well, see you then.'

He glances at my clothes, which cling to my breasts, then quickly looks away and crosses the road to his house. I enter the door code to my building and climb the stairs to my flat.

'Hello?'

I sling my keys onto the hallway table and move into the kitchen, peeling off my clothes as I go. I fetch a towel from the bathroom to dry my hair. Hopefully Nikki remembered to bring Marcel's toys in from the garden.

I crack the eggs into a bowl.

'If you're going to make an omelette, you've got to break some eggs,' I say to no-one

Whisking the eggs has me wondering what my neighbour is having for his tea. Our kitchen is at the back of the flat, but if I look out of my bedroom window I can see right into his house. I take the bowl through to my bedroom.

Johnny's iPad is laying on my bed and the duvet is rumpled and messy. I can always tell when my youngest has been in my bed because his iPad is out of battery and my duvet is bunched up into one corner of its cover. I plug in the iPad and shake out my bedclothes, smoothing them and making the bed look nice. It looks so nice I have to have a lie down.

It is dark when I wake up, and the rain has stopped. The street lamp outside my bedroom window has come on, but there are no lights on in my neighbour's house. When I go into the living room, John is there, sitting on the sofa in his school uniform with his iPad.

'Oh, you're here! Why didn't you wake me?

'You were asleep,' he says. 'What's for tea?'

'Omelette.'

I return to my bedroom to fetch the eggs. John and I eat our tea on our laps in front of the television. He tells me he plans to take up smoking because it made Walter Raleigh feel better while he was waiting for his head to be chopped off. My boy is a sucker for history. He tells me the executioner gave Raleigh's head to his wife, who carried it around with her in a little velvet bag.

'Would you keep mine?' he asks.

'Your what?'

'My head, if it was chopped off.'

'While all around men are losing theirs,' I reply, but he doesn't know Kipling's poem so I google it and make him recite it out loud with me until Lily bangs on the wall and yells at us to shut up.

'When did she get in?' I ask, and John tells me she's been home ages.

I knock on Lily's door to see if she wants anything to eat, but she hates omelette. I put the bubble gum on the floor outside her door, like the mince pie and sherry offerings she used to leave for Father Christmas when she was little.

Later, when the house is dark and the kids are asleep, I google Nikki's husband, the writer, and her father-in-law, the painter. Her husband's solemn expression on his publisher's website reminds me of Marcel. I find several pictures of him and Nikki at various literary events. In some of the pictures he sports a flamboyant moustache, and in one of the photos Nikki holds a cigarette. Across the road, Sameer's shop is still open, so I nip over and buy a packet of fags. I smoke one leaning out of my bedroom window. Across the road, my neighbour is home. I can see him in the lighted window of his house, dancing.

§

THE NEXT TIME I visit Marcel, I can hear a terrible wailing.

'Dog – don't be alarmed,' Nikki says, when she opens the front door. 'Rob usually takes him to the office, but he hasn't left yet – he wants to meet you. He's a pain in the arse, if I'm honest,' she whispers.

I'm not sure if she means her husband or the dog.

She leads me into the living room where Marcel lies on a sheepskin in the middle of the floor. The contrast of his dark hair against the whiteness of the room and the white fur rug is striking. He looks like a raven chick in snow.

Nikki's husband is sitting at the old-fashioned writing desk, but gets to his feet as we enter. He is a giant of a man, towering above his wife and me. He has a shock of wild, sandy-coloured hair.

'Here she is, the woman of the hour!' Nikki says. 'Bobbi, this is my husband, Rob; Rob, this is Bobbi.'

She falls briefly against her husband, laughing, and he gently pushes her away so she stands upright once more. He holds out one of his enormous hands for me to shake.

'Are you a Roberta?' he asks.

His voice is as deep and resonant as an opera singer's.

'Sorry?'

'Are you a Roberta or is Bobbi your given name?'

'Given, yes,' I tell him.

In life I can't see any resemblance between this man and his son. When we drop hands he rubs his hair vigorously and smooths it behind his ears.

'Can I pick him up?' I say, indicating Marcel on the floor.

'Oh god, yes – do!' Nikki says. 'Otherwise someone might tread on him!'

I kiss Marcel hello. He smells of oats and yeast, with a tang of sheepskin. He smells of nature. I breathe him in.

'Now you've met the help, you can get off to work,' Nikki says to her husband.

She winks at me and downstairs the dog lets out a prolonged howl. Behind the house, a train slows to a halt.

'10:17,' Rob says.

'I'll get the 10:40,' Nikki says.

In the basement, the dog continues to complain, so she goes downstairs to release him.

'I like your ink,' Rob says, gesturing at my tattoo.

'Thanks.'

We stand opposite one another, his child in my arms. Neither of us know what to say.

'Is your office nearby?' I ask.

'Just around the corner. To be honest I could work from home, but the concentration's not so good here, especially with this little chap to distract me.'

He takes Marcel's hand and pumps it up and down on the words 'this', 'little' and 'chap', and we are saved from another awkward silence by a clatter of claws on the wooden floor as a German Shepherd bounds into the room. It buries its head in my crotch.

'Sorry,' Nikki says.

I nudge the dog away with my knee.

'What's its name?'

'This is Pinch.'

'It's from Shakespeare,' Rob says.

'We were planning to get another one and call it Bottom,' Nikki says, 'but one dog is enough, so the joke kind of ran dry.'

'*One* dog is too much, to be honest,' Rob says.

Marcel twists in my arms, looking over one shoulder and then the other, following the movements of the animal whirling around our legs.

'Now, Bobbi,' Nikki says, grabbing Pinch's collar. 'We had a think about what you could do with Little Lord Fauntleroy here and we wrote out a provisional timetable...'

As the dog tugs at her arm she manages to snatch a piece of paper from the old-fashioned writing desk and hand it to me.

'Provisional only,' Rob says.

'Can you take this hound?' Nikki asks him. 'I need to go.'

On the piece of paper there is a list written in elegant, looping handwriting.

10:00 – 12:00 playgroup/activity
12:00 – 12:30 bottle/nap
12:30 – 1:30 playtime
1:30 – 2:30 lunch
2:30 – 3:30 park/activity
3.30 – 4:00 bottle/nap
4:00 – 5:00 playtime
5:00 – 6:30 supper

Marcel has a handful of my hair gathered in his fist, ready for our swishing game. A swishing game could last for hours, which will throw out the timetable we have been given.

'Is that do-able, do you think?' Nikki asks.

She fetches a smart coat from the hallway and comes to stand in the living-room doorway to put it on.

'This is do-able,' I say.

'Lovely. And it would be helpful if you could write stuff down, you know? What he eats, when he poos, what time he sleeps. That would be a real help.'

She attaches a lead to the dog's collar and hands it to Rob.

'Bye bye, bunny,' she says, turning to Marcel and me. 'Have a wonderful day!'

She kisses him and her perfume hangs in the air around us for a moment. Then the front door slams and the sound of her heels on the pavement grows fainter.

'I'd better be on my way too,' Rob says.

He straps a soft leather satchel diagonally across his body then pats his chest, his hips, as if he has lost something.

'You'll need a key,' he says.

He digs inside his pocket and hands me a key on a plastic fob, which has a photo of a man walking a gigantic rooster on a lead. It is warm from his jeans and the caption underneath the photograph reads 'This Man has a Giant Cock'.

For our morning activity, I take Marcel upstairs to his parents' bedroom and we rootle through their drawers and wardrobe. With Marcel propped up against Indian embroidered cushions on the bed, I model his father's jackets in front of the mirror. They are enormous on me. A leather satchel hangs on the back of the bedroom door, newer and smarter than the one Rob left the house with. There is nothing inside it. I strap it diagonally across my body and put on a deep voice.

'Daddy's home,' I say.

Marcel stares at me and looks a little disapproving, so I

take off his father's clothes and we try on Nikki's necklaces instead. Marcel looks like a Hindu god in them, but he doesn't like the feel of the jewellery against his skin, pawing at the necklaces to get them off, so I wear them instead.

Downstairs, we study the art work on the walls. The paint rises off the canvases like cake icing. Life seems to bulge under the surface, as if the figures are bursting to get out and run around the room. I hold Marcel up in front of one of the pictures.

'Your grandad painted this,' I tell him, and I stroke his fingers across the textured surface.

'Is that a man or a lady, do you think?'

We trace the dark figure standing in the background of the painting.

'Is it a mummy waiting to see her baby, do you think?' I whisper, but his head feels heavy and I realise he has fallen asleep. I sit on the sofa and watch his back rise up and down in rhythm with my breathing. I listen to the trains pass by the back of the house while he dozes. A faint tremor announces each one, making the window frames rattle slightly.

Marcel sleeps for almost an hour and then, with a slight shiver, he stirs and lifts his head. He smiles at me and a lightness runs through my body.

'Hello, sweetness,' I say. 'Hello, Pickle.'

I feed him a bottle. I am still wearing his mother's necklaces and he fingers them while he sucks. After milk, I put him in his buggy and we go to the park.

The park has been re-designed since I came here with my children. John and his friends used to climb on the roof of the bowling-green clubhouse, but someone set light to it and now there is a patch of burnt ground where it stood. The generation who play bowls is dying off, so the bowling green has been given over to 'meadow maintenance'. A notice pinned to the low metal fence carries information about the seeds that have been sown. Wild flowers will grow here in summer. In the playground, palm trees next to the sandpit make the place look something like the beach in the photograph hanging in Nikki's hallway. We head to a bench where we sit and watch parents sifting sand through their fingers and burying their feet. Older children rush around the space, swarming over the climbing frame, shooting down the slide. Marcel sits on my lap, a still centre amid all this activity, his body resting against mine.

A woman enters the play area, carrying a little girl on her hip and steering a buggy with her free hand. She fastens the gate behind her and parks her buggy next to Marcel's.

'Gorgeous day,' she says, threading her child's limbs through the holes in the moulded plastic seat of the swing. She gives the swing a push and her little girl leans forward, staring at the ground as she sweeps forwards and backwards.

'Hot, isn't it?' the mother says. She takes off her cardigan and hooks it over the frame of the swing. 'I can't believe it's so warm. The weather's gone mad.'

'Climate change,' I say.

'Yes! Nature's all topsy-turvy.'

'I like your necklaces,' she says, eyeing Nikki's jewellery. 'They look good all together like that.'

'Thanks.'

'How old's your little boy?'

She assumes Marcel is mine and I don't correct her. After all, for the hours we are together he is mine. He is mine and I am his.

'Six months.'

'She's nearly a year, but I've got a twelve-year-old too,' the other mother says. 'Bit of a gap!'

Her little girl rocks back and forth, legs dangling.

'I think I recognise you,' the woman says. 'Have we met before?'

'I don't think so,' I say.

'Your face is familiar,' she insists. 'I'm sure I know you.'

'Maybe we've seen each other here,' I say.

John is twelve – I probably pushed him side by side with this mother's older child on these same swings, but I don't tell her that. Instead, I tell her it is time for me to go and she tells me to have a nice rest of my day.

'What's for dinner?' John asks when I get home.

My children are toe-to-toe on the sofa, heads bowed over their devices.

'How about a takeaway?'

They can't believe their luck. I phone for a pizza and when the delivery guy buzzes at the door I pay him with notes from the old-fashioned 'wages' envelope Rob handed me when he came home. It has my name written on it in the same writing as the timetable, misspelled with an 'y' instead of an 'i'.

What my children don't know is that the pizza is a trade for the visit I want them to make tomorrow.

'I'm going over to Gran's in the morning, will you come? I thought you could use her for your art project, Lils.'

'What about John?'

'He came last time. It's your turn. She won't be around forever – one day you'll want to see her and she'll be gone.'

We open our pizza boxes. Lily plucks at a piece of mozzarella with the delicacy of a harpist.

'I'll pay you,' I say.

'How much?' John asks.

'No, forget that.'

Pizza is one thing, but to offer money feels wrong.

'I'll give you something. You can choose.'

Lily looks at me and points a half-chewed pizza crust at my blouse.

'Done.'

Later that evening, when I undress for bed, I knock on her door.

'Here's that blouse,' I say.

Her room smells warm and dry and papery. She is sitting in bed writing out Shakespeare quotes for her mock. Fluorescent pink and yellow Post-it notes decorate the walls. I lay the blouse on the end of her bed and she lifts her sweatshirt over her head. She gets out of bed and puts on my top. As she twists this way and that in front of her bedroom mirror, I can see my own reflection behind hers, and when she moves in front of me, her face eclipses mine, a facsimile of mine; mine a worn version of hers. She glances at me in the mirror, shy because she is pleased with how the blouse looks on her. As we study our double reflection, our bodies seem inseparable, as when I was pregnant with her. For a brief moment I have difficulty telling one of us from the other, like I did when she was tiny, in those first weeks after her birth when it was unclear for each of us where my body ended and hers began. She is so pleased with the blouse that she reaches behind her and takes my hands, placing them around her waist. She traces my tattoo sleepily with her fingertips like she did when she was little, and the expression on her face is not dissimilar to my rosy-cheeked Babushka, whose smile carries a sense of the love she has for the smaller dolls on her insides.

§

THE NEXT DAY we catch a bus over to my mother's. The unusually warm weather has given way to a colourless sky and Lily shivers at the bus stop in my blouse.

Mum lives in sheltered accommodation on the outskirts of town. We get off at the ring road and walk a little way to her block, calling hello as we let ourselves into her flat. She is sitting in her armchair in the living room with her aged dog, Little Legs, on her lap.

The television volume is turned up loud. Mum offers us her cheek to kiss.

'You smell nice,' I say.

'Eh? Let me put this off, wait a minute.'

She fumbles for the remote, which Lily hands her.

'What did you say?'

'Your hair smells nice, that's all.'

'My dog's got no nose,' she says, and she pokes Lily in the ribs but Lily doesn't know the joke.

'How does he smell?' I say.

'Terrible.'

She pats Little Legs and tells him she doesn't mean it.

'Lily wants to draw your portrait, Mum.'

'Homework, is it?'

'You have to sit really still.'

'I 'ain't going anywhere.'

Mum tips Little Legs off her lap and smooths her skirt,

which could do with a wash. Lily clatters around in the kitchenette, gathering up a packet of gravy granules, some liquid soap, an old-fashioned biscuit tin decorated with a picture of chrysanthemums.

'We're meant to draw the person with things that represent them,' she explains.

She assembles the items on the hostess trolley next to her grandmother's armchair, picks up Little Legs and puts him on her grandmother's lap once more. As she starts sketching, I put away the clean washing I've brought with me. Sheets, towels and underwear fill the drawers to the sound of Lily's pencil scratching.

'How are the children?' Mum asks. 'Are they doing well? Are they thriving?'

'I'm fine thanks, Nan,' says Lily, and her grandmother look surprised at the sound of her voice, as if she had forgotten she was there.

Once all the washing has been put away, I move into the bathroom where I scrub the tiles and bleach the yellowing rim of the toilet. The extractor fan whirrs while I polish the mirror my mother probably looks in every morning - does she still look, I wonder? And if she does, does she recognise herself there? My own face is close to the glass as I work. I breathe on the mirror, then rub it with my cloth to shine it. Is there something of Mum's reflection left behind the glass? Or inside it, maybe? Merging with mine now as I rub and rub?

When I have finished, I fill the kettle in the kitchen and make three cups of tea, arranging some biscuits on a plate. Lily is pleased with her drawing, even though she admits it doesn't look like her grandmother.

'It looks like someone, though, doesn't it?' she says. 'That's the main thing.'

She holds out her pad and squints at the portrait.

'It looks more like you, Nan, if you look at it like this,' she says.

Meanwhile, Mum is studying a biscuit, turning it round and round in her hand.

'Are you going to eat that?' I ask her.

'It's got something in it,' Mum says, pointing at the hole in the middle of the chocolate ring.

'It's a hole,' I tell her. 'It's a biscuit with a hole in it. A ring, you know?'

'No, in the middle, see? There's something.'

'It's like a Polo, you know? The mints?'

'Mince?'

'It's nothing – the something you can see is nothing – look.'

I put my finger through it and wiggle it at her, hold it up to my eye like a monocle and peer at her through it. I want to make her laugh, but she gives a little sigh and shakes her head. For a few moments she looks baffled and then she is herself again. Except she's not. She hasn't been herself for a while.

Lily adds to her drawing, sketching the window behind Mum's head, and through it, a view of the hedge bordering the communal garden, stretching away in perspective. The line of the window bisects the page and it looks as if Mum has a stalk growing out of her hair or an alien's antenna. I make the mistake of saying so and Lily scribbles all over her drawing and announces she is ready to go.

'How are the children?' Mum asks when we say goodbye. 'Are they thriving?'

Lily kisses her, but she looks right through her as if she is a ghost. Whenever I leave her, I don't know who will be here next time I come. Will it be Mum, or will it be the strange, vacant little lady who sometimes sits in her armchair? The one with stains on her skirt. I am gripped by an anxiety that perhaps she won't be here at all, so I pop in to see Jacqui, who is the manager of Mum's block and lives on the ground floor. Lily huffs and puffs, complaining that we have been here too long already.

Jacqui is watching the news and has half an eye on the television while I tell her about the biscuit with the hole in it.

'She's getting confused about really normal things,' I say.

'My mum was the same,' Jacqui says. 'She barely knew me by the end. Just go with the flow, that's my advice.'

'But if our own mothers don't know us, how can we know ourselves?'

Jacqui doesn't have an answer, she tells me to put my trust in God.

'It's out of your hands,' she says.

When we get off the bus Lily wants money for sweets. I hand her some coins and she disappears inside the shop. My neighbour is crouched at the side of the road, a little way off.

'What have you found?' I ask.

In the kerb, a tiny furry creature lies curled in on itself, eyes closed.

'Baby squirrel.'

'Is it dead?'

'I don't think so. It must have fallen out of its tree.'

We both look up into the branches of a tree that clatters buses going past.

'I'm thinking of moving it, in case a dog gets it or something.'

'Go on then.'

He puts down the litre of milk he is carrying and hands me a bunch of keys. He cups one hand and, with the other, scoops the animal gently into his palm.

'Now what?'

'Have you got a box? We could take it to a Squirrel Rescue Centre.'

'Is there such a thing?'

'Bound to be.'

We go inside the shop and ask Sameer if he has a box he can give us.

'I could get a towel or something to make it more cosy for the little fella,' my neighbour says, and together we cross the road to his house. I wait on the pavement holding the Wotsits box with the baby squirrel in it, while he unlocks his front door and goes inside. A smell of fresh paint wafts through the open door and I can see a bike helmet hanging on an empty coat hook.

He emerges after a few minutes and tucks a towel inside the box.

'My van's this way,' he says.

We walk around the corner. Someone has leaned an old mattress against a wall with a hand-written note attached: 'Take Me'.

'Is the little fella ok?' my neighbour asks.

I lift the corner of the faded yellow towel inside the box and tell him I think he's alright.

His campervan has checked curtains at the windows and there is a small sink and hob in the back. A collection of maps is tucked next to the driver's seat. I sit in silence with the box on my lap while my neighbour searches for local animal rescue centres on his phone. When he has found one he starts the engine and hands me his phone which has our route marked out.

'Head straight onto the main road,' I say, and he does.

The young woman on reception wears a pink tabard with the rescue centre logo on its breast pocket. She has pink varnished fingernails and dyed pink hair.

'Aw, it's only a baby!' she says when she looks inside the box. 'Leave this little guy with us.'

'If it's alright with you, we'll wait,' my neighbour says.

'It'll be a while before it gets seen,' she says.

'Have you got a lot of patients, then?' I ask.

'We're always busy,' the receptionist says, and she invites us to take a seat. Then she gets up from her desk and disappears into a back office taking our squirrel with her.

'What do you call a baby squirrel?' my neighbour asks.

'How about Nutkin?'

'No, what's the correct term, I mean.'

He googles it on his phone. 'Baby squirrels are called babies or infants while in the nest.'

The receptionist returns and sits behind her desk. Her fingernails tap noisily on the computer keyboard. Then a door opens and a young woman in veterinary overalls crosses the waiting area to where we are sitting. Her overalls have the rescue centre icon on the breast pocket and her white rubber shoes squeak on the shiny floor.

'Are you the couple who brought in the baby squirrel?'

'We are,' says my neighbour.

'Will it survive?' I ask.

'There's a good chance it will,' says the vet. 'Thank you for bringing it to us. We'll keep it hydrated, check nothing's broken, and when it's strong enough it will be released back into the wild.'

'It's too young to be released, surely?' I say.

'We'll care for it here until it's strong enough to look after itself.'

'You've got cages out the back?'

The young woman frowns slightly.

'I don't follow . . .'

'Cages where you keep all the squirrels and badgers and things?'

We ask if we can see where the animals are kept – as if we are parents considering a boarding school for our child. The vet tells us the public are only permitted to see the animals on designated open days. She asks the receptionist for a leaflet listing the Open Day dates and her shoes squeak noisily as she goes over to the desk. A look passes between her and the pink-haired woman as she takes the leaflet and squeaks back across the waiting area to hand it to us. We make a donation towards the cost of our squirrel's rehabilitation and drive home.

'Well, thanks,' I say when my neighbour has parked the van. 'That was . . . interesting.'

'Yes.'

He pulls a 'sad' face, as if to acknowledge that we did what we could and there is nothing more we could have done.

'I'll be seeing you,' I say.

'I expect so.'

Outside the shop, Sameer is flattening cardboard boxes for collection. He looks at us but doesn't say anything. I step off the kerb to cross the road. When I look back, my neighbour is chatting with Sameer and I know he is telling him about our squirrel.

§

'I THINK I'VE got a new man,' I tell my mother the next time I see her.

As much as anything, I am testing out the sentence to see how it sounds.

I like the way it sounds.

'I see,' Mum says. But she doesn't really.

Her hair is un-brushed and her clothes look as if she put them on in a hurricane. A ready meal stands on the kitchen counter, cooked and still in its plastic tray, untouched. There is a knife and fork and an empty plate next to it, as if someone was prepared to eat it or someone prepared it for Mum to eat it. I don't know who prepared it. It could have been Mum or it could have been Jacqui.

'You didn't eat your dinner, Mum,' I say.

'I don't feel like it.'

'But what about last night?'

'I didn't feel like it then either.'

I make her a jam sandwich cut into triangles like the ones I used to make for John and Lily's lunch boxes when they were small. She devours it, her face muscles working fast. I make her another one and she eats that, too.

'How are the children?' she asks, but I know she doesn't know who I am.

'Are they thriving?' she asks.

I miss her, even though we are in the same room. Is it

foolish to want so badly to be present in the mind of another? My mother affirms who I am – she is my mother, after all. She made me. I try going with the flow like Jacqui has told me, but our exchanges grow more and more outlandish. When I am putting away clean washing she tells me the queen dirtied her towels.

'Did she? The queen? She's like that, so I've heard.'

'Dirty hussy,' Mum says.

I am losing her. She is not the woman I knew. She is someone new.

§

FOR ONE OF his 'activities' Nikki asks me to take Marcel to a baby signing class.

'If he can learn to communicate with us, it will stop all the un-necessary crying,' she says.

'Babies cry,' I tell her. 'It's what they do.'

'Only because they can't make themselves understood,' Nikki says. 'See what you think. It's fun – I think you'll enjoy it and you get a croissant at half time.'

The class is held in a church hall in the middle of town. Nikki has phoned ahead to say I will be bringing Marcel. When I arrive, I am greeted by a woman in a yellow sweatshirt with the word 'instructor' on the back who shows me where to park my buggy.

Lily used to come here for Brownies. Brown Owl invited us to a ceremony where a round piece of cardboard covered in silver foil was a pond and we were told to close our eyes and imagine we were in a forest glade.

'Twist me and turn me and show me an elf.

I look in the mirror and I see . . .'

Lily was meant to say 'myself', but she got a strop on and Brown Owl had to say it for her.

The instructor invites me to join several other women who are sitting on the floor in a circle, holding babies on their laps.

'Who's Me-Signing today?' the instructor asks, and she introduces each child by singing their name and making a gesture with her hands that corresponds to its rhythm. The adults repeat her actions and words.

'Have we got Mar-cel?' the instructor sings, and she makes the shape of a letter 'M' by lifting her elbows and inverting her hands, touching her fingertips together. The other mothers sing Marcel's name and copy the instructor's gesture.

I am so busy learning everyone's names and gestures I forget to teach Marcel how to make the signs. There are songs to learn, too – traditional rhymes with some of the words changed:

'Ring a ring of roses, a pocket full of poses, a-tishoo a-tishoo, we all make signs'.

'It's important to interact with your child like this at home,' the instructor says. 'So you can teach them the new signs we're learning each week and better understand what your babies are trying to communicate.'

After half an hour of singing and signing, she announces a break and the women gather their children and get to their feet, moving over to a serving hatch where coffee is being served from the adjoining kitchen. Only one other woman and I remain on the mat. She wears a headscarf and her baby is called Jasmine.

'No coffee for you?'

Jasmine's mother gestures at the queue. She and I sit in silence watching the crowd of other women laughing and chatting until it is time to resume signing.

During the second half of the session, the instructor works with a hand puppet.

'Birdy says wel-come Mar-cel!'

'Birdy' has goggly eyes, yellow feathers and an orange plastic beak. Marcel tenses in my lap and shrinks away from the creature. I hold him close while the instructor jabs the air around us. 'Silly Birdy,' I whisper to him when she moves away.

He falls asleep in his buggy on our way home and stays asleep even after I bump the buggy up the steps and bang the front door shut.

'Home again, home again, jiggety jig!' I sing, in the style of the signing instructor, but he still doesn't wake up. His eyes are closed, lips gently parted. His breath is barely detectable, even when I hold my ear next to his mouth. I whisper one of Lily's Shakespeare quotes in his ear:

'This feather stirs, she lives!'

While he sleeps I roam the house poking in corners and idly looking through drawers. I try on Nikki's coat. There is a packet of chewing gum in the pocket. I take one and chew it noisily like a teenager, watching myself in the hallway mirror.

In the old-fashioned writing desk in the living room I find neat stacks of stationery - brown wages envelopes like the one my money comes in, white envelopes and notepads of all shapes and sizes. I flick through the pages of one of the notepads. The paper is good quality, cream-smooth on one side, slightly rougher and faintly ridged on the other; the kind of paper someone might use to write a love letter or an invitation. I take a silver pencil out of a pot of pens and pencils. It has a rubber in the end, like a small pink teat, and is surprisingly heavy.

'Surprisingly heavy,' I say out loud, weighing it in my hand.

When I twist the nib, the lead of the pencil extends. I write Marcel's name on the creamy paper.

Marcel.

I write John and Lily's names.

I rub out the names but their imprint remains. I tear out the page and fold it into neat squares, put it in my back pocket.

The 16:40 slows to halt behind the house, its brakes hissing and squeaking.

I twist the nib of the pencil, extending the delicate lead until it snaps.

§

I FIND EXCUSES to go to the shop in the hope I will bump into my neighbour. I haven't seen him since our trip to the animal rescue centre. One evening I am rewarded – I am standing at the till when I sense him behind me, but I don't look round and at first he doesn't say anything. I can't help glancing at him as I am about to leave.

'Hello, you,' he says.

'Oh! I didn't see you there!'

He knows it's not true.

'Dessert?' he says, eyeing the tin of custard in my hands.

'Always.'

'And there's me with just biscuits,' he says, showing me the packet of Fox's Fingers he is holding.

He is very good-looking. I like the way his grey hair shows up the blue of his eyes. I think I will call him Silver Fox.

'Wait for me,' he says, 'I want to show you something.'

Sameer hands him his change while I wait at the open door. Outside the shop, he picks a free local paper out of the wire rack and shows me an advert he has seen for an open day at the animal rescue centre.

'We could go if you like,' he says.

'They'd only show us any old squirrel and tell us it's ours.'

'I guess . . . ok, then.'

Later, when I am smoking out of my bedroom window, I can see him ironing in his bedroom. He hasn't closed his curtains, even though it is late. If he looked up he would see me, but he doesn't look up. His arm sweeps from side to side, gliding the iron over a shirt. If he looked up I might wave, but he keeps his head bowed over the ironing board. I wave anyway and then I stub out my cigarette, let myself out of the flat and cross the road in my bare feet.

'Were you ironing?' I ask when he answers the door.

'I was.'

'I could see you.'

He looks me up and down – there is no need for him to undress me with his eyes because I'm not dressed, I am in my nightie.

'I feel bad for crushing your dreams,' I say.

'My dreams?'

'About going to see our squirrel.'

He takes my hand and pulls me gently across the threshold. He shuts the door with a click and in the freshly painted hallway we press our bodies together, one against the other.

§

IN THE FREE newspaper there is also an advert for a city farm. They have a lambing pen that is open to the public and I ask Nikki if it would be ok for me to take Marcel.

'Of course,' she says. 'He loves animals.'

I trundle his buggy up and down wooden walkways between pens. Several ewes have given birth and lambs only a few hours old lie damp in the straw.

My phone pings. It is a text from the silver fox.

I had fun last night x

Then another message follows.

How bout you?

I text back.

I had fun too x

One ewe in a corner pen is making a lot of noise.

'See a baby being born?' I ask Marcel and I wheel his buggy over to where a mother sheep is in the final stages of labour. Her sulphurous orange eyes stare wildly and she throws back her head to tear the air with a terrible shriek.

'mmmmeeeeeaahh!'

Marcel bursts into tears, but with the mother's yell a moist yellow lamb, slithery with amnion, spills onto the straw.

'Look, Marcel! Baby sheep!' I say, but he is inconsolable and I have to take him over to the other side of the barn. I park the buggy next to an enclosure of older lambs.

Me at city farm x

Nice x

My phone pings with a donkey emoji. I send one of a sheep.

Before we leave, Marcel and I check on the ewe. She is quiet now, and motionless, as is her lamb, which is underneath her, with just its knobbly yellow back showing. I'm worried it will suffocate.

'A mother over there is sitting on her baby,' I tell one of the farm workers. 'Is that ok?'

The farm worker is a young woman with a mean face. She tells me the lamb is fine. Marcel and I return to our vigil. When the lamb bleats from underneath its mother its raucous sound makes us jump. The mother sheep shifts her great weight and begins to clean her baby of the yellow gunk that covers its body. Fox sends an emoji of a cute penguin. I send him a steaming turd.

§

'WHAT WOULD YOU say if I had a boyfriend?' I ask my children.

They are on their devices while I write in the diary I am keeping for Marcel, in which I record the signing sessions, our trips to the park and city farm.

'I wouldn't like it,' says John, not looking up from his iPad.

'Have you, then?' Lily asks, studying me.

'I don't know.'

She announces she is going to change her name.

'What's your new one going to be?' her brother asks.

'I was thinking May.'

'And may we still call you Lily?' I ask her.

'You may,' says my daughter, 'but I probably won't answer.'

'No change there, then,' I say, and she pulls a face.

John wants to hear the story of how we named him and I tell him once again about the way his father and I talked about him when he was in the womb, calling him 'John' as a kind of joke. Once he was born we couldn't think of him as anything else so John he became.

The door buzzer goes. I get up to answer it.

'Too fast!' John complains. 'You told it too fast!'

'It's me,' says Fox over the intercom. 'I texted you.'

'My phone's charging.'

'I could see you in your flat. I was waving.'

'I didn't see you.'

'You weren't looking.'

'No.'

There's a pause.

'Fancy coming to mine?'

I glance into the living room.

'Not tonight.'

'Washing your hair?'

'Something like that.'

I tell him I'll come down. When I reach the bottom of the communal stairs he is pressing his face against the glass door, squashing his nose, distorting his features.

'I just wanted to see you,' he says when I open the door.

'And now you have.'

'Now I have, yes.'

He points his toe over the threshold. Lily would mock him for his trainers.

'You can't come up,' I say.

'Too soon?'

'Yes.'

He shushes takeaway leaflets with his foot.

'And you don't fancy coming over to mine?'

'No.'

I try to soften my refusal with 'thank you', but it's too late. He tells me that's fair enough and you can't blame a guy for trying. I watch him cross the road. He glances back at me when he opens his front door. I wave at him, silhouetted in the bright rectangle of his doorway, and he waves back.

I go upstairs.

'Mum, can I have hair extensions?' Lily asks.

'No.'

'Loads of girls at school have them.'

'Why would you want someone else's dead hair on your head?'

'All hair is dead hair,' she tells me.

'Not while it's growing out of your head it isn't,' John says.

She picks a strand from her own head and holds it up in front of his face. 'Dead,' she says.

Later that evening, a pile of belongings materialises outside her bedroom door – a heap of clothes, a jewellery box, the doll's house we bought her for her birthday and a diary with a tiny gold padlock.

'What's all this?' I ask her.

'Things I don't need any more,' she says.

§

I AM TUCKING Marcel into his buggy after a signing class when I spot a poster on the wall calling for child-minding volunteers. The image on the poster is a simple line drawing of a baby's face with a squiggle for its hair and a dimple in each cheek.

Jasmine's mother is waiting for me so I quickly write the number on the back of my hand with a biro. Ama laughs to see me struggling to get the pen to work on my skin. Her English isn't very good so our relationship is mostly based on laughing at one another.

We wheel our buggies down to the park and sit side by side on a bench while our babies sleep. We don't talk much, which suits me. Our exchange is limited to a sign language we make up as we go along, yawning and laying our heads on our hands to show how tired we are, rubbing our bellies when we are hungry, tapping our wrists when it is time to leave. She hasn't commented on my tattoo, but then again, why would she, she doesn't have the language with which to comment. She hasn't mimed surprise at it, though, and it is quite an unusual tattoo. I'm not sure they have Russian dolls where she comes from. When I want to express surprise that the park isn't busy, I exaggeratedly stare around me and wave like the queen. Ama seems to understand, nodding and smiling. I ask her whether she lives with a partner, drawing a house in the air and pointing at Jasmine then conjuring a shadowy figure to sit next to Ama on the bench and lifting my eyebrows in the shape of a question. Eventually she grasps my meaning and is able to communicate that her husband is at work, cooking in a busy restaurant, judging by her mime. When the babies stir, we push them on the swings for a bit and then we say goodbye and go our separate ways.

The garden is in full sun after lunch so Marcel and I sit on the front steps of the house, on the shady side of the street. He is bigger now and the noises he makes are different, closer to speech, perhaps. He is trying to copy the noises he hears people making around him. I draw a baby's face in chalk on the pavement for him, trying to get him to make a 'b' sound.

'Baby!' I say. 'Ba-by.'

I draw several baby faces, but can't seem to capture the beaming joy of the one on the poster at the church hall. Something about the shape of the squiggle I draw for his hair isn't right and the two lines for his dimples are in the wrong place. Over and over I draw it and soon there are several beaming baby faces on the steps leading up to the house. We are drawing a line right to the end of the street and back again when Rob arrives.

'Pinch needed to go,' he says, gesturing with the plastic bag that dangles from his fingers.

He plops the knotted plastic bag on the pavement and sits on the steps with us.

'Scorchio, isn't it?' he says, getting a hanky out of his pocket and wiping his forehead.

He tells us he can't concentrate in this heat, the words won't come. He takes Marcel from me and bounces him on his knee.

'This is the way the gentlemen ride! Trit-trot, trit-trot, trit-trot.'

Marcel chuckles so Rob whooshes him above our heads and holds him there, his little boy's arms and legs splayed like a flying squirrel's. If his daddy lets go, Marcel would bounce down the steps like a rag doll.

'I like your street art,' he says, handing his son back to me.

He tiptoes along the line we have drawn in an exaggerated way, like a clown walking a tightrope.

'Right, playtime's over,' he says when he has completed his chalk walk.

He scrabbles his hair with both hands so he looks like a mad professor, then smooths it down again with the flat of his palm and whistles to Pinch, who is busy rootling through the neighbour's recycling boxes.

'I wish I could spend the day hanging out with you guys,' he says.

I tell him he's welcome to hang with us and he asks me if I mean that and tells me I am fun.

'Is there a man in your life, Bobbi?' he asks. 'Anyone special?'

'No-one special, no.'

'Shame,' he says. 'He doesn't know what he's missing.'

He whistles for Pinch once more, but the dog has disappeared inside the neighbour's driveway and he has to go and fetch him. Marcel and I watch them walk away, following the line we have drawn. Then we go indoors, seeking the cool of the house, taking Rob's bag of dog shit with us.

When I get home, I dig out Lily's old diary from the pile outside her room. Its pages are empty apart from one date she has decorated with an explosion of hearts and stars ('My birthday!') and some Saturdays marked with the word 'Dad'.

'Can I have this?' I ask her.

'What for?'

'Writing in.'

She shrugs so I consider it mine. Both kids are floppy in the heat. It's too hot in here, they complain, so I go around the flat opening all the windows, but there is no breeze, the weather is stifling. I sit on my bed in my underwear. The phone number I wrote on my hand has nearly rubbed off, so I ring it before it disappears altogether. A youth worker answers and when I explain about the poster I saw advertising for childminder volunteers he tells me about the support group he runs for young people who have experienced difficulties. Some of the young people have babies, he says, and he is hoping to find a childminder to look after them while the young people themselves take lessons in life skills.

'I could do that,' I say, doodling in Lily's diary.

'I'm afraid it's unpaid.'

'I don't mind.'

'And you'll need the appropriate clearances, of course.'

'I've got those,' I tell him, doodling away.

'Great!' the youth worker says. 'My name's Andy.'

He invites me to the next session. When our call is over I discover I have covered the first two days of the year in Lily's diary with baby faces.

§

I BUZZ THE buzzer and a young man opens the door.

'You must be Bobbi,' he says. 'I'm Andy.'

He tells me there's a dance class just finishing and as he speaks, a tide of little girls in black leotards and tap shoes flows past us. They are only young, perhaps four or five years old, but the force of them pushes me backwards and my body is pressed against the door. I hold out my hand and their neat hairstyles skim my palm.

'Mind, girls!' calls one of their mothers.

She apologises to me, rolling her eyes. The dance teacher is packing up her stereo. Taps on her shoes clack as she moves backwards and forwards on the parquet floor, unplugging the machine from the wall socket and gathering up paperwork, stuffing it into a gym bag.

'Sorry, I'll be out of your way in a minute,' she says.

'No worries,' Andy says.

He turns to me, pointing out several buckets dotted around the room.

'Bit of a roof issue,' he says.

The door buzzer goes and he leaves, returning moments later with a young woman pushing a pram. He unbolts the double doors and I help prop them open so she can wrestle her pram into the space.

'This is Bobbi, one of our volunteers,' Andy tells her. 'Bobbi, this is Keji.'

The young woman wears an old-fashioned skirt and blouse. Her hair is plaited in short braids, parted in sections.

'Girl or boy? I ask, gesturing inside the pram.

'A boy. Oladimeji.'

Her voice is very soft.

'And how old?'

'He is just four months.'

Keji picks her child out of his pram and I give his booteed foot a little tug.

'Do have your . . . ?' Andy asks.

Keji and Andy watch me as I dig inside my bag for the child safety and criminal conviction certificates I have brought with me. Then the door buzzer sounds again and Andy takes them with him. He returns with a young woman and her little boy and hands me back my certificates.

'Who have we got here?' I ask the boy, who looks about two years old, with a round face and a mad-monk haircut.

'This is JD,' his mother says.

She wears a black T-shirt and black leggings and bandages up both arms.

'Hello, JD.'

I offer the boy my hand, but he squirms out of reach, hiding behind his mother's legs.

Andy arranges chairs into a circle in the middle of the room and more young people arrive: two skinny young men in grey hoodies and grey tracksuit bottoms, and three young women holding babies. One of the women nods at one of the young men and he follows her across the room to sit next to me. She is small and pale and wears her hair in a high ponytail.

'She's burning up,' the woman says, tugging at her child's doll-sized denim jacket

'It is hot in here,' I say. 'There was a dance class before.'

'That's why it stinks,' she says.

'Sweaty Betty,' I say, and she laughs.

'Yeah! Sweaty Betty is right.' She unthreads her baby's little arms from the sleeves of the jacket.

'Need a hand?' I ask her.

'Nah, you're alright.'

'Alright, Jade?' the young man says, once the operation is finished. He reaches out to tickle the baby's tummy. She is wearing a pink all-in-one with the words 'Daddy's Girl' written on it. Her skin is so pale that delicate veins are visible at her temple. She has a surprising amount of hair for such a small baby. It is like a doll's hair – a cloud of fine, blonde curls, which look like gold under the community centre lights. The young woman passes this dandelion-doll to her partner and folds then re-folds the tiny jacket, smoothing it out on her lap.

Andy wants our attention.

'Thank you for coming,' he says when everyone is seated. 'This is Bobbi. She's here to look after your children, if you want her to, while you're in the life skills sessions.'

Some of the young people look at me, but mostly they stare at the floor.

'What do we think?' Andy asks. 'Could that be helpful to any of you?'

'Not being funny, but they're all kiddy fiddlers,' the mother of 'Daddy's Girl' says.

She looks at me.

'No offence,' she says.

'None taken.'

Her partner bounces their baby vigorously on his knee.

'No way am I handing her over – some of them lot are paedophiles.'

The baby's legs bob up and down with his movements.

'Do remember that anyone working for youth services has clearance,' says Andy.

'That don't mean nothing,' the young woman says and taking her baby from her partner, she stands and begins to pace the room.

'I ain't got time for these fuckers who hand their kids over at the drop of a hat,' she says. 'Why'd they go and have a kid if all they want to do is get rid of it?'

It's difficult to tell how old she is, but my guess is that she is only sixteen or seventeen. The other young people follow her with their eyes as she walks up and down in the middle of the circle. It is impressive, the way she holds everyone's attention. The only person who won't look at her is her boyfriend, who stares at the floor.

'Hey, Andy!' she says. 'Did Connor tell you he landed a job?'

'Did you, Connor? That's excellent.'

'Well dodgy, if you ask me,' says his girlfriend. 'Unpacking lorries at some random warehouse. Still, make a change from playing the X-Box all night, won't it.'

'Biggest kids of all, aren't they,' says the woman with bandaged arms. She shouts at her little boy who is busy paddling his hands in one of the buckets dotted around the room.

'JD! Dirty!'

Andy wants to get back to the issue of childcare. It might be something to consider, he says, if you young people get jobs.

'I got a job,' says the young woman with the ponytail, and

she gives a shrug to indicate the little body humped over her shoulder. 'She's my job. I'm her mum. That's my job.'

'What if you wanted to go out to work?' Her boyfriend asks, and the young woman falters for a moment. Standing still in the middle of the circle of chairs, she concedes that yes, she could see that there might be a time when she would need childcare. Andy nods encouragingly.

'And what kind of thing would you want to know about the care on offer?' he asks.

'I'd wanna know if she was going to be safe,' she replies.

§

THE ROOM IS dark and the air is thick with a sweet, rancid smell. Mum is curled on one side in her bed. She is panting – faint, shallow gasps. Little Legs has been banished to the other room where he lies on his special rug next to Mum's empty chair.

'The doctor's been,' Jacqui says. 'I didn't know if you'd want a priest?'

I shake my head.

'Her life's in His Hands now,' Jacqui says. 'I'll leave you to say goodbye.'

She bustles out of the room, whispering 'God Bless' as she goes.

I sit on the bed and take Mum's hand. It is cool to touch, its yellowish skin stretched thinly over the bones. It grows cooler in mine as I massage her knuckles, like worry beads or a rosary. Soon the birds are waking up and light is seeping in from the corners of the sky. There has been a night but I didn't notice its passing.

'I hope you haven't been playing that all night,' I say to John when I get home.

He ignores me, and on the TV at the foot of his bed, a zombie advances, eyes bulging. John's hands fidget the controller and on the screen he angles his weapon. The volume is turned down because he knows I can't stand the noise. The only sound in the room is the clickety clack of his thumbs on the controller.

'Nan died,' I say.

John blasts another zombie. It evaporates in a spray of gore then springs mercilessly back to life.

'Did you hear what I said?'

He switches off the television and pats the bed next to him like I used to pat mine when he was little. I climb in and lie down, close my eyes.

'Poor Nan,' he says.

His duvet smells of hay.

'Will I have to wear a suit?'

'What?'

'To her funeral?'

Somewhere outside a bird is singing.

'I wish you'd read a book instead of playing those horrible games,' I say.

'I don't like books.'

He stretches across the bed to reach for something on the floor.

'Black holes distort the space around them, sucking up matter and creating a vacuum. The gravitational pull in a black hole is so great nothing can enter it, nothing can escape it, not even light.'

Without opening my eyes I know he is reading from the encyclopaedia of space that his dad gave him.

'During the death of a star, it grows and grows until it's enormous, then there's a massive explosion during which the star becomes as bright as a hundred million suns and all that's left is a black hole.'

'Well that's cheered me up no end.'

'Dad says half the atoms in our bodies are made outside the Milky Way.'

'Don't believe everything Dad says.'

He holds out a hand, turning it over, examining it, musing on the fact that bits of him have been blasted out of a different galaxy.

'All this talk of Galaxies and Milky Ways is making me peckish,' I say. 'Will you go to the shop?'

He ignores me, returning to his book and reading aloud about the absence at the centre of our universe. Then he lays the encyclopaedia aside and is quiet for a while.

'If you think about it, words are meaningless,' he says at last. 'What do they even mean? They're just words to say what we don't really know.'

I think about Jacqui and her religious faith and I close my eyes once more.

'Don't let me fall asleep,' I say. 'I have to be at work in a few hours.'

'Words don't really matter, do they?' he says.

'Matter doesn't matter,' I reply, sinking into sleep.

I wake up late for my shift with Marcel.

'Don't worry,' Rob says when I phone to apologise. 'I'm in no hurry to get to work.'

I catch a cab.

'Whose are the flowers?' I ask the driver as we pull up outside.

Several bunches of flowers rest against a lamppost. The driver doesn't know. He stares at the 4×4s in the driveways and the ornamental trees in pots as I fumble in my purse for his fare.

'You made it!' Rob says when he opens the door.

I hang my bag on the banister and we head down to the

kitchen where Marcel is waiting in his highchair. He kicks his feet excitedly when he sees me.

'Hello, my beauty,' I whisper, and he lifts his gaping mouth to mine.

His breath is warm and sweet, his cheek soft as suede.

Rob's laptop is open on the table. He snaps it shut and puts on a crumpled linen jacket from the back of his chair.

'I'll be off, then,' he says, rubbing his hair in the distinctive way he has, scrabbling it vigorously and smoothing it behind his ears.

'Uuh, uuh,' Marcel says, and I pluck him out of his highchair.

Rob whistles for the dog and all of us go upstairs, Pinch pushing eagerly ahead, thwacking me with his tail as he rushes past. Rob opens the front door and when he bends to kiss Marcel goodbye, he hesitates slightly, as if he might kiss me, too.

'Whose are the flowers?' I ask.

Rob glances across the street and tells me a young boy crashed his motorbike, smashed his head in. A thick smell of diesel wafts into the house on the warm breeze and I feel faint.

'Are you alright, Bobbi?'

'Sorry . . . I feel a bit—'

He takes Marcel and makes me sit on the stairs.

'I'm ok . . .'

'You're not going to swoon on me?'

From the station, the brakes of a train let out a high-pitched wheeze.

'My mum died last night. I'm a bit . . . I didn't get much sleep.'

'Oh no, Bobbi! Why didn't you say?'

'It's alright – it wasn't unexpected.'

'All the same, that's massive. You don't need to be here – we can cope.'

'No, really, I want to – this is where I want to be.'

I stand again, holding out my arms for Marcel, but Rob insists I take the day off.

'We'll pay you,' he says, handing me my bag.

Then he goes into the living room and returns with the money Nikki has left for me in one of the old-fashioned wages envelopes.

'Call it compassionate leave,' Rob says.

He shuts the door after me and I cross the road to read the messages written in the cards attached to the motorbike boy's flowers. *Forever in our hearts.*

§

FOX SAYS HE can't reach me.

'But I only live across the road,' I say.

'You won't let me in,' he says. 'You're a closed shop.'

We are at his, in bed as usual. Or rather, I am in bed and Fox stands in the doorway, naked. In the bathroom, the taps are running.

'I've never been inside your flat.'

'Not much to see.'

'You've told me so little about you.'

'Nothing to tell.'

He raises an eyebrow at me as if to say he thinks otherwise. I ask him to teach me how to do it.

'How to do what?'

'One at a time – look, I can only do both.'

I lie in bed raising and lowering my eyebrows at him.

'Stop trying to change the subject.'

I lift the duvet, inviting him back to bed. but he stays where he is.

'That won't work either,' he says.

'Are you sure?'

The smell of our bodies rises up from under the bedclothes. Fox fixes me with his blue eyes. and after a few moments he leaves the room, calling me from the bathroom to come and join him.

'Let's go on a date,' he says. 'A proper date.'

We are in the bath now. He has the end with the taps.

'Where do you want to go?'

'Somewhere people go on dates. The cinema? A restaurant? I could take you out for dinner.'

It's too hot in the bath. I get out and stand dripping on the bathroom mat.

'My mum died.'

Fox is looking at me. She died, I tell him. It wasn't unexpected, but if I seem distant, that could be why.

'You should have said something.'

'I am saying something.'

'You can tell me anything,' he says, staring down at his penis which floats gently in the water. 'I'm here.'

I stare too, and I know he knows something. Someone has talked. One of our neighbours. He draws his knees together as if to protect his softest parts from me.

'Sorry if I was pushy,' he says.

He runs the cold tap, cupping water in his hands and sluicing it over his face.

'You don't need to apologise,' I say.

I sit on the toilet. The hot water has relaxed my sphincter, but if I go home to use the toilet, he will accuse me of holding back, of being unreachable. I pick up one of the wildlife magazines he keeps on the windowsill and flick through the pages, reading aloud snippets from an article about two dolphins called Hector and Han.

'When their trainer makes the sign for 'tandem' they are able to communicate with one another to agree on which stunt they will perform'.

'Maybe they're not communicating,' Fox suggests. 'Maybe they're just really fast at imitating each other – so fast that humans can't detect it.'

I ask him if he is a scientist now and he tells me no, he read the article, that's all.

'Dolphins are incredibly social animals,' he says. 'A dolphin on its own isn't a real dolphin.'

'Who wants to be real?' I ask him.

'Don't you?'

'Just real enough.'

'How real is real enough?

'This real,' I say, as my bowels empty.

He can't help a look of disgust flicker across his face. This is what happens when I don't hold back.

§

LILY'S DIARY IS filling up. I have written about Mum's dying and about Fox's wanting.

It all gets written down, even his floating penis.

I write about Andy arranging for the young people to do a pottery-making workshop as part of their life skills project.

'What's pottery got to do with life?' one of the young men in tracksuit bottoms asks.

'Creativity is important,' Andy tells him.

'Fuck that,' says the young man, untying the laces on his trainers and retying them.

'We're just asking you to give it a go,' Andy says.

He gets some plastic sheeting out of a cupboard and asks for help bringing in some tables from another room. JD's mother and Connor carry a table between them. Her arms aren't bandaged tonight, revealing the bloodied dashes which score them from wrist to elbow.

'Alright?' Connor says to her as they set the table down.

'Alright,' she replies, and she stretches her arms out in front of her, palms upwards, blowing on the scabs, as if to cool them.

Connor's ponytailed girlfriend Kim jiggles their baby on her lap. She doesn't take her eyes off Connor.

While his mother is helping with the preparation of the room, JD fits shapes into the holes in the top of a toy post-box. The toy belongs to the community centre and black felt-tipped letters denote it as community centre property. Most of its shapes are missing and the colour has rubbed off so it is pale pink instead of pillar-box red.

Soon everyone is seated behind tables laid out with Plasticine and clay. JD goes to sit next to his mother who is stirring a mixture of plaster of Paris and water.

'The idea is to have fun,' Andy says. 'Have fun!'

Some of the young people attack the materials straightaway, rolling long sausages out of Plasticine and holding them against their bodies, swinging them from side to side like enormous dangling penises but others cry out to Andy 'this is boring' and 'what are we meant to do?' The women complain their nails will get dirty.

I ask Kim if she would like me to hold Jade.

'Be my guest.'

She passes me her child and shakes her empty arms.

'Cor, that's better!' she says, turning to Connor with a grin that lights up her face. 'Right, where we goin'?'

He gives his Plasticine penis a vigorous whirl which sends the end of it flying across the room.

'You bell end!'

JD is up off his seat once more, racing Connor to snatch up the stray body part which he gives to his mother. Nat eyeballs Connor as she squishes the plasticine in her fist.

Jade fits neatly in the crook of my arm. She is warm with the heat of her mother's body. I stroke the veins showing through the skin at her temples and Kim catches me.

'Weird them, aren't they?' she says. 'Doctor says they're normal, reckons they'll go when she's bigger.'

'She's gorgeous,' I say.

When I stroke Jade's sticky little palms, she flexes her fingers and curls them around mine.

'Love it when they do that,' Kim says, studiously ignoring Connor and Nat.

'Me too.'

While Andy spends time at each table asking the young people what they want to make and offering suggestions, I walk Jade around the space.

'Watch how they're showing each other their work and taking it in turns to look after each other's babies,' Andy whispers to me when Jade and I have completed our rounds. 'Wonderful.'

Kim says she is making a doll of Connor so she can stick pins in it if he fucks her over. I pull up a chair at her table and sit next to her. By the time the session is over, their baby is asleep in my arms. Kim checks to see if she still has hold of my finger – she does, and Connor tells me I've got the magic touch. Kim takes Jade from me and tucks her into her pram, which is lined with a lacy pink cushion decorated with miniature bows and gold appliqué unicorns.

'What a beautiful cushion,' I whisper as Kim lays her gently on top of it, fluffing out the lace around her head so she looks like Thumbelina in a flower.

'Connor's sister gave it to her, didn't she,' Kim says.

Keji's baby is asleep too. I hold the door open while the young women wheel their children out of the building.

'Well that was a success,' Andy says as he and I begin to tidy up the room.

We are sweeping bits of Plasticine and clay from under the tables when there is a tapping on the window. Connor ducks out of sight when Andy looks up, but he signals that he wants to speak to me. I go outside to the car park where he and Kim are waiting.

'We're looking for someone to have Jade so we can have a night out,' he says.

'I thought you weren't keen, Kim?' I say. 'Last week you said—'

'That was last week,' he says. 'She changes her mind like the wind, this one.'

'If you need someone, I'd be happy to babysit,' I tell them.

'Have her at yours?' Kim asks.

'If you like.'

'It'll cost us though,' Connor says.

'I'd do it for free.'

'Legend!'

I tell them not to mention it to Andy – something tells me he wouldn't approve.

'Free country,' Connor says. 'She's our kid, it's up to us who looks after her.'

I give them my address and we arrange for them to bring Jade the following Saturday. I watch them wheel her away in her pram and then I go back inside where Andy is laying out the pottery shapes on sheets of newspaper.

'Look at this,' he says.

He shows me what Kim has made: a small clay baby and a cradle for it to sleep in.

§

JACQUI TELEPHONES. SHE needs me to empty Mum's flat. She has another occupant waiting. When I arrive, Mum's name has already gone from the doorbell. The windows in all the rooms are open and a breeze whips through the place.

I sit in Mum's chair to drink the coffee Jacqui makes me. A trolley containing cleaning equipment stands in the middle of the room.

'She enjoyed living here,' I say. 'Thank you for all you did for her, Jacqui.'

'You're most welcome. Mary was a wonderful woman.'

She stands with her rubber-gloved hands on her hips and surveys the room, making a mental note of all the jobs she wants to tick off. Little Legs pads around the place looking for someone who isn't here.

'She's no place you'll find her,' Jacqui tells him.

'I'd like you to have something of hers,' I say, looking at Little Legs.

Jacqui looks at him too. She has been feeding and walking him since Mum died.

'A piece of jewellery or some kind of keepsake, you mean?' she says.

Jacqui takes off her rubber gloves to go through Mum's treasures with me. I show her a brooch in the shape of a book, a souvenir of the Lake District where we went camping a few times. Its pages are made from real paper, each featuring a scenic photograph. They unfold like a concertina. Jacqui and I look through the miniature photographs.

'I've never been,' she says. 'It looks nice.'

'If you wear this, the Lake District goes where you go.'

Jacqui bursts into song. 'I've been to Paradise but I've never been to me!'

The catch on the brooch is weak so the covers of the book can't contain its tiny pages and they spill out. Jacqui chooses a gold cross on a gold chain instead. She puts it on straightaway and then she puts her rubber gloves back on and fills her bucket with hot water. She wants to make a start on the bedroom.

Fox is pleased when I ask him to help me move Mum's bits and pieces. I have arranged for most of the furniture to be collected by a house-clearance guy Jacqui recommends, but I want to keep the dining table she never used and some crockery she did.

And then there is Little Legs.

'Funny little guy, isn't he?' Fox says. 'What kind of dog is he?'

'The loving kind,' I say.

It feels exposing to take Fox inside her flat – the place looks shabby and Little Legs is kind of odd-looking. It takes us a while to manoeuvre the table into the van. Afterwards, we carry boxes and bin bags outside and arrange them on the forecourt. It is bright and windy and a pub sign further along the road creaks as it swings back and forth. Something in the strong breeze and the quality of light takes me back to my childhood. I stand with my mother's possessions gathered around my legs and I am ten years old in the Lake District with her and Dad unpacking the car around me. The tent in its bag, our clothes in holdalls, food supplies and cooking equipment in cardboard boxes – a miniature version of our life packed into the boot to be unpacked and re-located to a field somewhere. A sign creaks in the wind and the sun is in my eyes, Dad is shouting at me not to stand there like an idiot and Mum is busying herself so he doesn't get annoyed. Maybe some of the very same items are in the bags and boxes here on the pavement. The catch on my mother's souvenir brooch has come unfastened and the book unfolds concertina-like down my body. I re-fold its pages and tuck them inside, re-fasten the catch.

'This lot for taking?' says a voice.

The House Clearance guy. Fox tells him yes and he swings a bin bag over each shoulder and throws them into the back of his van. Another man emerges from the vehicle. He is sorry for Fox's loss. Fox thanks him without telling him the loss is mine. The House Clearance guy casts an eye over Mum's belongings.

'Looks like you've got some nice bits here,' he says.

One of Mum's neighbours passes slowly along the street pushing a wheeled shopping trolley with a tartan cover. Mum used to call her The Duchess on account of her weekly trip to a hairdresser instead of using the mobile service that visited residents in their homes. She pauses on her journey and points at Mum's armchair.

'Is that going begging?' she asks.

The seat cushion bears the imprint of my mother's body.

'It's spoken for,' says one of the House Clearance guys, as he and his partner lift a chest of drawers into their van.

'I could do with a chair like that,' says the old woman.

'You can have it,' I say, but she has continued on her way and can't hear me. She is startled when I tap her on the shoulder.

'You can have the chair,' I say.

I have to repeat myself several times.

'It's yours,' I say, mouthing my words exaggeratedly so she can lip-read.

Her face brightens and for a moment she looks eight instead of eighty. Fox and I lug Mum's chair back along the street.

'Where are you taking it?' asks one of the House Clearance men. 'That's a good chair that is – it's the best piece.'

'I've found a home for it,' I tell them.

'It was promised to us,' the man says.

'What are you going to do with it?' Fox asks.

'We'd find it a good home,' the man says.

'We've found it a good home,' Fox says.

'We'd give it to someone who really needs it.'

'We're giving it to someone who needs it.'

'It's a good piece, that is,' says the man forlornly.

Fox and I go back inside Mum's flat where Little Legs is lying in his bed. He is the only living thing in the flat. He is the only thing in the flat. I gather up his bed with him still in in and carry him to Fox's campervan.

'Want to take a few moments?' Fox asks, but I tell him I've had enough moments and he nods and starts the engine. We drive back across town and outside my building he waits while I take Little Legs up to my flat to introduce him to his new home. I need help getting Mum's table up the stairs, though. We wedge open the communal door with takeaway leaflets and a telephone directory and we tip the table onto its side to carry it between us

'Who uses a telephone directory these days?' I ask.

I am talking for the sake of talking – about telephone directories and about the best Indian takeaways, about anything and everything. Outside the front door to my flat he waits while I get out my key then slides the table forward a few inches.

'I don't want to scratch it...' he says, gesturing for me to take the other end.

We carry the table carefully inside. Fox tries to hide the quick looks he darts around the place, trying not to be intrusive on this first visit to my home. I wonder how much he knows. Someone has talked.

We back the table into the living room doorway so he can squeeze around it to get into the kitchen. He does a double-take when he sees the tins of custard crowding the shelves and surfaces.

'I guess you like custard?' he says.

'Love the stuff.'

'Me too.'

He removes the fruit bowl, putting it on the draining board and lifting the flimsy old Formica table out of the room. I park it in the hallway next to the pile of Lily's things outside her door. I can sense Fox trying to work out the geography of the flat, trying to assess which room is mine.

'It looks good,' I say, when Mum's table is in position.

It looks ridiculous. The polished dark wood is out of place in my scruffy kitchen. It was out of place in Mum's flat too, which is why she never used it. I pull up one of my cheap dining chairs and sit on it, spreading my palms on the table's smooth and shiny surface. Fox draws up a chair at the opposite end.

'Dinner?'

'Not yet.'

'Custard?'

I shake my head.

'But maybe one day? A guy can dream?'

His eyes are as blue as a swimming pool.

'Bobbi . . .' he says.

'I'm not ready.'

I escort him down to the entrance of our building and we kiss before he crosses the road to his house. Little Legs, acting as chaperone, follows us and now he hops back up the stairs to the flat with me, claws clicking.

§

'YOU'RE SURE IT'S not too soon?' Nikki asks when I phone to say I am ready to come back to work.

'Positive,' I say. 'Spending time with Marcel is the best cure.'

I run there, and I am sweating by the time I arrive. I can't help banging noisily on the door. Marcel seems pleased to see me, smacking my face and pulling my hair when Nikki passes him into my arms.

'Gentle! Gentle!' she tells him and she takes him from me.

'Watch this,' she says.

She places him on the kitchen floor and he twists his little body around and tips himself onto all fours, scampering eagerly away.

'He's on the move!'

'He thinks he's a dog,' Nikki says, as Marcel heads towards Pinch's food bowls. Pinch comes out from underneath the table, herding him away like a sheep dog.

'Soon he'll be walking and talking,' I say.

'Oh, and there's another thing,' Nikki says.

She places both hands on her belly and looks at me.

'Sooner than we planned,' she says.

'Congratulations.'

'Thanks. We were going to wait but, well . . . What's the gap between yours?'

Unbreachable, I want to tell her. The gap between my children is one that cannot be breached.

'Three years,' I say.

'Oh, quite a big gap,' she

'Quite big, yes.'

Once she has left I whizz Marcel fast down the hill in his buggy. Eeeeeeeyyy! Little Legs needs walking and Marcel loves dogs. Also, he will be interested to see where I live. It's a change of scenery for him.

'When the new baby comes they won't want you any more,' I tell him. 'You'll have to come and live with me.'

I key in the door-code and wonder if Fox is home and if he is watching. I bump Marcel's buggy up the stairs with him in it, counting each step out loud. When I open the door, Little Legs is there to greet us.

'Look, Marcel! Look what tiny legs he's got!'

It feels strange to have him in my territory, seeing what he makes of the sights and smells. He is unimpressed by Little Legs so I show him Lily's doll's house, but he crawls off to investigate the kitchen. I follow him on all fours for a Marcel-eye view and he thinks I am chasing him. I let out a ferocious growl and he moves fast, squiggling his way under Mum's table to get away from me. He watches me from under the table, excited and nervous at the same time. I take oranges from the fruit bowl and roll them to him across the sticky floor.

My home must feel like a doll's house to him, being so much smaller than the one he is used to. When I coax him out from under the table I show him my bedroom. We bat the dreamcatcher hanging from the ceiling and blow its feathers but Marcel is too sophisticated for such play now and squirms to be released. After a tour of the living room I fetch poo bags and lead and the three of us trek back across town to the park.

Dogs aren't allowed in the playground so I park the buggy

next to a bench on the path and we watch Little Legs sniff among the flowerbeds. A man in dark clothes emerges from one of the tents pitched in the bushes. He ambles over to us and I wrap my arms tighter around Marcel. Little Legs sniffs at the frayed hems of the man's trousers.

'What a gent,' the man says. 'What an absolute gent.'

He asks what his name is.

'He's called Little Legs.'

The man has three tears tattooed next to one eye. John once told me a teardrop tattoo means the person has killed someone and this man, sinewy and tanned, looks capable of such a deed.

'Ha! I've only got little legs too, mate!' he says. 'Look at them!'

He dances a few steps.

'Jack Russell?

'Sorry?

'Reckon he's got a bit of Jack Russell in him, that one, and a bit of sausage dog, too.'

'You might be right.'

'Talking of sausages, money for a cup of tea?'

I give him a pound coin.

'Tea's one fifty,' he says.

I give him another coin and he wanders off. Little Legs follows him along the path until I whistle and he comes back.

After the park we head back to Marcel's. I can barely get inside the door because an enormous double buggy, wrapped in clear plastic, fills the hallway.

'I went shopping,' Nikki says.

It is a struggle to get Marcel's buggy inside so she hauls

her new purchase into the living room out of the way. She is excited by its mono and duo variations, with expandable carrycot and seat facing world options. We remove the wrapping and Nikki invites me to hold its leatherette handlebar and pinch the air tyres.

She wants to know what Marcel thinks of his new chariot so we sit him in it, but Marcel has only just got out of a buggy, he doesn't want to be strapped into another one. He starts to complain, writhing and arching his back. Nikki gets him out again and sets him down on the floor among packaging printed with warnings to keep away from young babies and animals.

She asks if I would mind helping her clear the cupboard under the stairs. Feeling queasy, she has taken the day off work so Marcel and I won't be by ourselves. He weaves around my feet with Pinch, who sniffs among the tennis rackets and camping equipment I pull out of the cupboard. Nikki makes herself a cup of ginger tea and drinks it on the patio where she can supervise Marcel and stop him eating the plants.

It takes me an hour to clear enough space for the new buggy. When I have finished, I wheel it into the cupboard and Nikki comes to inspect my labour. We stand side by side and stare at the two empty seats.

'It feels weird,' she says. 'Knowing Marcel will be in one half and not knowing who will go in the other . . . Knowing there will be someone to fill the space but not knowing who it is.'

She places her hands on her belly and I think how adorable Jade would look sitting next to Marcel in the posh new buggy.

'I kind of want a girl,' Nikki says. 'It would be nice, wouldn't it?' She shakes her head, quickly brushing away tears. 'Oh dear, bit hormonal,' she says.

§

ON SATURDAY, KIM arrives punctually at six o'clock. Jade is crying.

'Hungry,' Kim says. 'She's due a bottle.'

She wheels her pram into the foyer and we take Jade out. Her cries echo in the stairwell. Kim hugs her tight, bouncing her up and down and shushing her while I bump the pram up the stairs. The woman across the landing comes out of her flat.

'It's alright, she won't keep you awake, she don't cry at night,' Kim tells her.

'You can't leave the pram on the landing, it's a fire hazard,' the woman says.

'I'm taking it in,' I say, and the woman goes back inside her flat.

'I'll give her fire hazard,' Kim says.

Little Legs comes to the door to greet our guests.

'Alright with kids, is he?' Kim asks, bending down to let him smell her hand.

'He's fine. Hardly a pit bull, is he?'

Kim laughs.

She sits at my mother's table to feed Jade her bottle and I sit next to her. Jade's little hand waves in the air, like a sea creature wafting in a current. I give her my hand and she wraps her fingers around mine. All three of us are connected, four if you count Mum.

'Nice place you've got,' Kim says, looking around as if she is casing the joint. 'Better than my shithole.'

Jade's eyes gaze around the room like her mother's.

'What's with all the custard?' Kim asks.

'I'm going through a custard phase, that's all.'

'Nothing wrong with custard,' Kim says.

'Would you like a drink?'

'What have you got?'

'Tea? Coffee?'

'Nah, you're alright.'

We wait for Jade to finish feeding. Afterwards, Kim holds her over her shoulder to wind her and I bend close, whispering nonsense about unicorns while we wait for her dainty burp. Kim laughs at my stories and tells me I'm mad.

'Not the full ticket, is she Jade?' she says, kissing her child and handing her to me.

'Loves her bath and she loves reading,' she says, talking me through Jade's bedtime routine. 'She's even got a book you can read in the bath – I packed it in her bag.'

She shows me the contents of the bag she has packed.

'Bottles and milk, look. Clothes for tomorrow, clean nap-naps for her bum-bum.'

She holds up a tiny pair of trainers.

'How cute are these? Connor got them for her, but they're a bit big.'

She puts the shoes back and gets out a pink elasticated headband with a pink flower, which she pulls over Jade's curls before stashing the bag under the pram. As we move to the door she glances at a framed photograph of John and Lily but doesn't say anything. She kisses Jade, telling her to be good. When she has gone I take Jade into my bedroom and we stand at the window watching the sunset.

'Red sky at night,' I say, and I explain to Jade something John once told me, which is that that shepherds' delight is a result of pollution. The unicorn cushion in her pram is a bit grubby and smells of fags, so I take off her things and put them all in the washing machine, singing as I go. I lay her on a folded towel on the bathroom floor and sing her a song about Jade going Jogging in her Jeggings while I run a bath.

'Off comes Bobbi's top – peek-aboo!'

She blinks with astonishment at my naked body. I show her my tattoo, tracing its outline and telling her about the smaller dolls inside her, telling her about the plan I have for Lily and John to have matching tattoos of their own, if they want them, of course.

'Lily's would be slightly bigger, on her forearm,' I say, showing Jade on my own body what I mean, 'and John could have an even bigger one, on his bicep, maybe – then when we hold them next to each other they'll make a family of dolls.'

She studies me closely, looking from my tattoo to my face and back to my tattoo again, reaching out to touch it with her tiny doll fingers. I tell her about all the ladies in the world that she could grow up to be and she understands everything. Maybe she'll have a tattoo one day.

The water is womb temperature and we are like twins, the little one contained within the bigger one. Jade likes the noise the water makes when I fill an empty shampoo bottle and hold it up high, pouring out its contents. I hold the bottle higher then lower and we listen to the different notes, thundering when there is a gush, petering out to a tinkle as the container empties. I pour the water over her head and it straightens out her curls. She looks quite different with her hair long and wet, gathering like seaweed on her mermaid shoulders.

After our bath, we lie wrapped in towels on my bed under the dreamcatcher. With her small face peeking out, she looks like an Inuit baby or a little nun. I scroll through images of gemstones on John's iPad, showing her pictures of jade. Some pieces are pale and cloudy like milk, others are as glassy and bright as boiled sweets. I pluck at these bright images and bring my fingers to my mouth, smacking my lips loudly, pretending to eat them.

'Sweeties! Yum yum!' I say.

Jade lets out a laugh. It's not often that she makes a noise – she rarely cries and I haven't heard her laugh before, so I do it again and again until she decides it's not funny anymore.

Some of the jade has been carved into faces, of laughing Buddha, of stern Chinese emperors, of a Mayan God who visits earth in the form of a parrot and whose job it is to bring up the sun every morning and take it down again every night.

'Time for beddy-byes,' I tell her.

The sky is dark now and there are lights on in Fox's house. I send him a text:

Look who I've got x

He comes to his bedroom window. I waggle Jade's little hand at him and he waves back. While I feed her a bottle I tell her about the golden-haired princess whose father boasts she can spin gold. I put her in my bed and I am the last thing she sees as she falls asleep.

I am woken a few hours later by a buzzing on the intercom. I stagger into the hallway to answer it.

'Bobbi! It's Kim and Connor! Let us up.'

'What time is it?'

'Let us up, can you?'

I buzz them in and they're on the stairs, swearing and shushing. Little Legs click-clacks to the front door of the flat and we poke our heads out, watching as Kim and Connor wind their way up to my landing. Connor is clutching his thigh and leaning on Kim, one arm around her shoulders.

'What happened?'

'Police were after us,' Kim says, panting. 'Connor's been stabbed.'

I hurry them inside the flat, whistle for Little Legs, who takes his time shuffling in after them.

'Fucking security guard had a knife,' Kim says. 'Got him in the leg, but it's not bad – we just need to get the blood off him.'

'What security guard?'

'Connor knows him from before. He was after the copper piping.'

'You can make loads on copper,' Connor says, limping into the kitchen.

'Let's have a look at that wound.'

'Nah, you're alright,' Connor says, smirking.

'Let her, Con,' Kim says, 'while I get the blood off.'

She tells him to take his boot off. They are Timberland style and one of them has a dark stain on the toe.

'It's evidence,' she explains, 'if the feds come asking. Give it here.'

'Never mind evidence,' Connor says. 'These are new.'

He sits at Mum's polished table and unlaces his boot with one hand, keeping the other clamped around his thigh. I hunt for the First Aid kit under the sink while Kim scrubs at the boot with the sponge I use for cleaning dishes.

'They'll be round tomorrow and this will be proof,' she says.

She is still panting.

'I'll wear my trainers,' Connor says.

'Of course you 'ain't gonna wear the boots!'

He rolls up the leg of his tracksuit bottoms, but the wound is higher up and I have to ask him to drop his trousers.

'Dirty cow,' Connor smirks.

He pulls them down, revealing Calvin Klein boxers and a skinny, hairless thigh with a deep gash in it. When I clean away the blood, a pale layer of fat is clearly visible inside the wound.

'You'll have to hide the boots,' Kim tells him. 'But they'll be checking under the bed, looking in your cupboards, trying to catch you out.'

'I'll ask Nat to look after 'em,' Connor says, flinching as I try to close the flesh together.

'Nat? Why ask that fuck-up?'

'Alright, then I won't.'

'No but why ask her? That's all I'm saying.'

'I'm not going to ask her! I'll chuck them out instead.'

'You can't chuck these out! They cost seventy quid!'

'Covered in blood...'

'I know they're covered in blood! What d'you think I'm doing? I'm cleaning them aren't I!'

They're shouting now.

'Careful not to wake Jade,' I say, and the mention of their daughter's name is like a magic balm.

'How was she?' Kim's voice softens.

She leans against the sink for a moment, catching her breath.

'Are you ok?'

'Asthma,' she says, placing a hand on her chest. 'Forgot my inhaler, didn't I. How was she?'

'She was perfect.'

I bandage Connor's wound, but it's deep and blood seeps through the dressing straight away. I tell him he needs to get it checked out at the hospital.

'Fuck that,' he says, and he turns to Kim: 'Are we going or what? I thought we were meant to be pulling an all-nighter.'

They take a look at Jade before they leave and Kim notices her things drying on the radiator.

'Thought I'd give them a wash,' I say and she nods.

We arrange to meet at the community centre the following morning.

'Take it easy,' I say. 'No more fighting.'

Connor laughs. 'We'll try.'

They disappear into the night. After they have gone, Little Legs comes out onto the stairs with me where I clean up the trail of blood with a baby wipe.

I wake to the sound of Jade shuffling around. Somehow she has worked her way to the end of the bed.

'Good morning, little lady,' I say. 'Good morning, my princess!'

She is warm from sleep and her hair is a blonde halo. With her flushed cheeks she is the prettiest baby in the world. We stand at the window watching day dawn while I try out different names on her. Aurora suits her, I think, and she seems to think so too. I make her a bottle and get her dressed in the little outfit Kim has packed.

She watches while I fold the rest of her clothes and pack

them in her bag. The unicorn cushion has come out beautifully in the wash, its gold stitching glints in the sunlight.

Kim is at the community centre before I am. She holds her cigarette behind her back and blows smoke over her shoulder as she crouches to greet her daughter.

'Spent all night at Nat's, didn't we,' she says when I ask after Connor.

'Nat as in Nat?'

'Yeah. She don't look after that kid of hers, y'know. He was awake the whole time we was there, running around the place.'

'I'm happy to have Aurora any time,' I tell her. 'Jade, I mean. I can have her any time you want.'

Kim straightens and tosses away her cigarette.

'I'll take her now, ta.'

I tell her about the double buggy Nikki has bought.

'Her baby's not due yet – We could put Jade in it, take her somewhere.'

'Take her where?'

'Oh, you know, the park.'

'Yeah, maybe.'

'I take the little boy to a singing group – Jade might like it.'

'She does like music,' Kim says.

'She does, doesn't she!'

I sing Kim the jeggings song and she laughs, tells me I'm a nutter. We arrange for me to take Jade to the next Me-Sign.

'What about your own kids?' she asks.

'They don't want to come singing with their mum anymore.'

'Growing up?'

I nod.

She doesn't need the truth.

§

FOX INVITES ME to lunch at a restaurant in town. I shave my legs and straighten my hair, put on my face. My earrings catch the light and the silk dress I bought for someone's wedding a few years ago clings to my stomach and breasts. I am pleased with my reflection in the mirror. Lily wants to know where I am going.

'Out to lunch,' I tell her and she says she knows that but where am I going.

'Funny girl,' I say. 'Which shoes?'

Lily shrugs so I limp into John's room wearing one strappy sandal and one plimsoll.

'Which shoes?' I ask, but he is playing on the X-Box and besides, his mother is wearing make-up and a sexy dress so he won't look at me. My phone is ringing and I hobble fast to the kitchen to answer it.

It is Nikki.

'I know it's short notice,' she says, 'but could you look after Marcel? Something's happened.'

'Is everything o?'

'My work is often not ok. Have you seen the news? We're the top story this lunchtime.'

I switch on the television and flick through the channels. A 'breaking news' banner running along the bottom of the screen informs me that a woman has been rescued from a house where she claims to have been held against her will for twenty years. Rob is at a meeting in London and Nikki needs me straightaway. I phone Fox to reschedule. He tries hard to hide his disappointment so I tell him about my strappy sandals and promise to go over to his afterwards.

'Don't bother,' he says, and I think I've blown it until he completes his sentence with the words 'wearing knickers.'

'Wow! You look gorgeous!' Nikki says when I arrive.

She already has her coat on and is in a rush to leave. Marcel is busy scrabbling at his crate of toys in the living room, trying to pull it out from the bookshelf. In his corduroy dungarees and mini flannel shirt he looks like a 1950s mechanic. When he sees me, he makes urgent noises and bounces up and down to enlist my help. The television is on, tuned to a news channel.

'Is it true?' I ask Nikki, dragging the crate of toys into the middle of the room. 'About the woman who was kept prisoner?'

'I'm afraid so,' she says. 'And she isn't the only one.'

She is busy texting someone but now she looks up from her phone.

'I have to speak to the press – do I look alright?'

She holds her coat open to show me her outfit – a neat black skirt and cream blouse.

'Very smart,' I say.

'You look amazing, Bobbi,' she says, noticing my silk dress as if for the first time. 'Is this how you look in normal life when you're not rolling around getting rice cakes in your hair?'

I tell her I had a date.

'Oh no! You're making me feel terrible,' she says.

She studies me for a moment.

'Gosh, I don't know anything about your life, do I? Well,

hopefully Marcel will appreciate how beautiful you look. Oh, and the dog, too – he's downstairs, if you could take him out for a poo?'

Then she is gone. Marcel and I empty his toys onto the living room floor but he soon tires of them so we pile up sofa cushions for jumping into. He is quite bold in his little body, even though he isn't standing on his own yet. I hold his hands and he knows to bend his knees before he performs a stunted little leap and lands among the pillows. His face is open with pleasure as he lies sprawled on the mountain we have made, laughing at the ceiling. I take a photo and send it to Fox.

two timing you with this little fella x

Marcel snatches at my phone, squawks to be thrown among the cushions once more. Pinch can hear us from his basement prison and starts howling, so we go downstairs and let him out. I sit Marcel on top of him and take another photo.

never work with animals or children x

I hold Marcel around his little dungareed waist and he rides the dog around the kitchen. After lunch, when he goes down for a nap, I phone Fox, putting him on speaker while I tidy up the sofa cushions.

'Looks like you're having fun,' he says.

'Are you jealous?'

'A bit.'

He asks where Nikki and Rob live. 'Up near the station, isn't it?' he says.

I tell him the name of the road and he wants to know the house number.

'Why do you need the number?'

'I'm in the neighbourhood,' he says. 'I could pop by.'

'I'm working . . .'

'I thought you said the baby was asleep?'

As we are speaking a text comes through from Nikki:

You missed a call from me at 14.49

Then another one:

R delayed, any chance u can do bath time & poss bed time?

'Bobbi? Are you there?'

'I might have to stay late,' I say. 'The woman I childmind for just texted . . .'

'Do they know about your situation, Bobbi?'

'My situation?'

'I know about your children,' he says.

A chill flushes through me. The silk of my dress feels cold next to my body.

'I know about your children,' Fox says. 'Sameer told me.'

I kill the phone call and run upstairs.

Marcel's room is dark. I stand in the doorway listening to his sleep-breathing. I like him to have a gentle waking rhythm. I crouch next to his cot and whisper his name, but he doesn't stir. His breathing continues, shallow and delicate, wispy as his hair. I speak his name a little louder and he gives a shudder, lets out a sigh. I reach inside the cot and slide my hands underneath his warm body, scooping him into my arms so I can rock rock rock him.

Downstairs, there is a knocking and Pinch starts barking. I take Marcel with me to answer the door.

'Hello, you,' Fox says.

'I'm working.'

'So I see – who's this handsome fellow?'

He takes Marcel's hand and tells him he is pleased to meet

him, but Marcel withdraws, half asleep and unsure of this stranger.

'You look nice,' Fox says to me.

'Thanks.'

He peers past me into the hallway where Pinch paces around in circles, whining.

'You can't come in,' I say.

Pinch comes to the door and Fox makes a fuss of him, stroking him and calling him 'boy' and telling him how handsome he is too.

'Don't let him out,' I say. 'How come you're here?'

'I was in the neighbourhood. What time do you finish?'

'I might have to give him his bath and put him to bed, his daddy's going to be late.'

'Do they know, Bobbi?'

Behind the house a train slows then stops.

'I think you should tell them,' Fox says.

The photographs hanging in the hallway tremble in their frames and the floor seems to ripple like a wave. It buckles and heaves and then is still once more. With a hiss, the train is on its way again.

'It's none of your business,' I say, and my voice seems unnaturally loud.

'No?'

He looks at me with his extremely blue eyes.

'No.'

I grab Pinch's collar and yank him inside the house.

'See you later?'

'Maybe.' I close the door and I can't help shivering with cold. Whose idea was it to wear a silk dress? I am shaking uncontrollably.

'It's alright, it's alright, shh shh,' I say, rocking Marcel and holding him tight.

We spend a quiet afternoon in the house. I'm scared to go out in case Fox is waiting for us.

'Did you get my texts?' Rob asks when he arrives home.

'My phone was switched off,' I tell him.

'Never mind. Sorry to keep you so late.'

He riffles through the stationery on the writing desk. 'What a day!'

'How was your meeting?' I ask.

'My meeting was good, my meeting was good.'

He gives up hunting through pens and paper.

'I've got your cash but I can't seem to find an envelope for it,' he says, pulling a wad of notes out of his jeans pocket. 'Sorry.'

'I don't need an envelope.'

Marcel wants to play with the pot of pens.

'Six hours, yes?'

'That's right.'

He separates five ten-pound notes, handing them to me.

'That's too much,' I say. 'I need to give you some change.'

He tells me to consider the extra a bonus for coming at short notice.

'What a day!' he says once more, messing up his hair then smoothing it behind his ears. 'Did you watch the news?'

He picks up the TV remote and aims it at the television, flicking to a news channel where Nikki is being interviewed in front of the Scotland Yard sign.

'Look, Marcel, it's Mummy!'

A red panel in one corner of the screen reads 'Live' and a banner underneath identifies Nikki as 'Charity spokesperson Nicky King'.

'Spelt her name wrong,' Rob says.

Marcel makes 'd' 'd' sounds and slithers off my lap, scampering on all fours over to the enormous television and pulling himself to standing. He thwacks the screen with a biro while his mother talks about highly traumatised women who have been rescued and taken to a place of safety.

'They're getting all the help and support we can offer,' she says.

'Dah, dah,' says Marcel.

'Mama not Dadda,' Rob says. 'Get that pen off him could you, Bobbi?'

The wind blows Nikki's hair in front of her face and she flicks it away. Rob thinks she looks nervous, but she seems very professional to me. I think about the baby growing inside her, invisible to viewers.

'She told me about the pregnancy,' I say. 'Congratulations.'

Rob nods.

'Thanks,' he says, not taking his eyes from the screen. 'Sooner than we thought but it'll be nice.'

His phone rings in his pocket. He checks the display and signals to me that he needs to take the call, mouthing Nikki's name.

'Yes, I'm here,' he says, leaning away from Marcel who tries to grab the phone. 'Yup, can do . . . Will do, yes . . . you just do your thing.'

The red panel on the television screen tells me his wife is speaking live, but she is on the phone to her husband. 'Live' isn't live.

'She might have to work all night,' Rob says when he has finished the call.

'I could stay if you like?'

He looks at me, taking in my silk dress and dangly earrings.

'That might be good,' he says.

'It's another pair of hands, isn't it,' I say. 'If you need help putting Marcel to bed – and in the morning.'

'As long as your own family can cope without you?'

I tell him they can cope.

'Thanks, Bobbi, you're a lifesaver,' he says.

He texts Nikki to let her know and I take Marcel upstairs to give him his bath. He is fat and shiny as a seal and bats enthusiastically at a family of yellow plastic ducks as they bob on the surface of the water. The ducks range in size from big to little and match the ones that decorate his changing mat. Occasionally he smacks them so vigorously that he loses his balance and slips under the water and I have to pull him to the surface again. I soap his little body then rinse him and lift him out of the bath and parcel him up in a towel. He smells of lemons. I write the words *Pick lemons* on the glass and Marcel and I watch beads of water drip from the letters. I take deep breaths of sandalwood and cinnamon and then I go downstairs.

Rob is sitting on the sofa with a glass of wine.

'I put a couple of ready meals in the oven,' he says. 'I hope you like Coq au Vin?'

He places his wine glass carefully on the floor, holding out his arms for Marcel. I give him his child.

'Careful he doesn't wee on you, he hasn't got a nappy on.'

'Oh wee away, boy,' says Rob. 'I don't mind.'

'There's something I should tell you,' I say.

Rob looks at me.

'Don't say you're pregnant, too?'

'No.'

The opposite, in a way.

The figures in the paintings on the living room walls seem to shift and stretch, as if readying themselves for some event or other. I can hear them breathing. I can hear them yawning and sighing. The floor trembles underneath me like the earthquake simulator John and I tried out in a museum once. I tell Rob my children died in a car crash two years ago.

'You're kidding me, right?'

He looks at me. I tell him I'm not kidding.

The words get easier, but other people's reactions are still hard.

'Oh, Bobbi.'

He sits back, his hands loosening around his own child.

Marcel squawks and kicks his legs excitedly.

'I'm so sorry,' Rob says. 'I'm so, so sorry.'

The strain in his face and voice are familiar. There was a time when I saw it in everyone's face and voice. *Sorry for your loss* hovers between us so I head up the stairs. In the bathroom, the words *Pick lemons* are still visible on the mirror, but the letters have dribbled. 'Pick lemons' was Lily's first proper sentence. She spoke it when we were on holiday in Greece and I wrote it on the back of the tourist map so we wouldn't forget. I lift the soap to my nostrils and I can smell the lemons we picked. I put the soap down again and fetch a clean Babygro and nappy from the linen cupboard.

'I don't know what to say,' Rob says, when I come back downstairs.

I am the walking wounded. My injuries are the empty

spaces around me which used to be filled with my children's bodies. They are plain to see, if you know to look for them. Fox knows to look for them and now Rob does too.

'It's ok,' I say.

'But it's not, is it,' he says.

He asks if I would like to talk about it and I tell him I wouldn't. They were with their father, I say, in a car he was driving. To spare us both, I tell him I will see him in the morning. I hand him the clean Babygro and nappy and I go upstairs. The wooden banister is smooth under my hand, the carpet caresses the soles of my feet. Each step seems to take forever.

§

THE TICKING OF a clock wakes me but I have no idea if I have been asleep for minutes or hours or days. I am still wearing my silk dress. I get out of bed and look out of the window. The street is dark and empty. Everyone is tucked up asleep in their beds. Tick. Tock. Tuck. With every passing second my children have been dead for longer, but it doesn't matter how long they have been gone, the point is they are gone.

Other people's pain adds to mine. A trip to the corner shop is agony: feeling my neighbours' eyes on me, the discomfort of Sameer's knowledge in every gesture of his, in every look. These are people who knew John and Lily, who saw them on their way to and from school, who pulled disapproving faces when they overheard Lily and her friends swearing, who told John off for kicking his ball over their fence or too near their car. Now they pull a different kind of face. They smile and say hello and some stop to pass the time of day, each of us aware of the empty space around us where my children used to be.

People were kind at the time, of course they were, but I couldn't take their kindness, can't take their kindness. They talked about my children being somewhere else. Above me, they said, or all around. I'm sorry, I would say, they are dead and when we are dead, we are dead, that is all. But they live on, don't they? In your memories, they would say.

We are born and then we die, that is all. The police made

me sit down when they came to the flat. They ushered me into my own living room like I was the guest, not them. The driver lost control of the vehicle, they said. The car was travelling at speed, they said, when it collided with the central barrier. All four occupants were killed on impact. 'Four occupants?' I asked the woman police officer, and she looked in her little black book and read out a woman's name I didn't recognise.

A woman died and I am jealous because she wasn't me. A woman who wasn't their mother was with them when the last air they breathed left their body. Her blood, her breath mingled with theirs when it was my blood and my oxygen while they were growing inside me, my bathwater they shared when we were trying to save money.

This isn't real, I said to the police. This isn't what I'm experiencing. I asked them to take me to the scene but they refused. I want to see where it happened, I said. I was there at the beginning and I want to be there at the end. Not a good idea, their counsellor said, Take me, I said. There's nothing to see. Of course there's something to see! Even if you're blind! Close your eyes and see what you can see, there's always something. A tree, a house, sky, like in the pictures Lily use to draw. A road. You police have no imagination, I told them and I saw one of them make a note in his little black book, the same as the woman police officer's, they all have them, to write down facts, only the facts, no imagination. Move along, there's nothing to see. Debris in the road and a bag of bloodied clothes they gave me when I asked.

I can't find the clock but its ticking is deafening so I get out of bed and creep along to Marcel's room. I stand outside the door listening for his breathing, but the ticking is too loud.

I go downstairs. My bag is hanging on the banister where I left it. I hook it over my shoulder and its weight is like a pendulum. It tips me slightly off balance, but I steady myself in front of the photographs lining the hallway walls. A streetlight outside shafts through the glass above the front door, lighting up Marcel's black and white portrait and the picture of the beach. The beach is empty and looks peaceful. It is somewhere I could go with Marcel.

The tiles of the basement kitchen are cold underfoot. I fumble for the light switch and when I find it their black and white diamonds swim in front of my eyes, their contrast too strident for this soft hour. Pinch is whining in the utility room so I let him out. He shows me where his biscuits are, his tail wagging. I pour them as quietly as possible into the metal bowl, but they rattle and clang.

The downstairs clock has a different tock to the ticking that woke me up – its deep echo in the empty room is calm and steady compared to the frantic chirping of the one upstairs. I unlock the tiny padlock on Lily's diary and start to write. I write about the clock ticking, about Pinch's biscuits. The flow of the words and the flow of the ink are aided by the rhythm of the clock which sets my pace.

As ink flows, so does my blood. There is a seeping in my underwear and when I go upstairs to the bathroom I discover I have started my period. I take off my dress and scrub it in the sink, turning the running water pink. I'm a poet and I know it. I can't find a tampon so I stuff my underwear with toilet paper. In Marcel's room, I stand in the doorway listening for his breath. The room is dark and still. I approach the cot, whisper his name.

'Marcel?'

But I can't hear him, can't see his shape in the dark. I switch on the light. The cot is empty. I run down the stairs, tap urgently on Rob and Nikki's bedroom door.

'Bobbi?'

'I can't find Marcel.'

There is movement in the darkness and a bedside lamp is switched on.

'He's here,' Rob whispers.

I can only just make out Marcel, asleep in a travel cot that stands next to the bed. I can see the soft round of his shoulder, his dark hair, that's all. Rob stares at me and I realise I am wearing nothing apart from the sexy underwear I put on for my date with Fox. It seems a long, long time since I was getting dressed for lunch. Now my knickers are stuffed with toilet paper and my dress is soaking in the sink

'Try to get some sleep,' Rob says.

I go downstairs in my bra and pants and shut Pinch in the utility room. Then I go back to my room where I lie down once more. The clock's incessant ticking fills my head. If I could see its face it might seem a friendly kind of clock, but I can only hear its torturous tick, each sound bisecting the dark into before and after.

It wasn't his turn to have them that weekend, but he wanted to take them to a luxury spa. He was flash with his money and he knew I had none, which was why we went on holiday together. John and Lily were confused. 'How come Dad doesn't live with us anymore?' they asked. 'Tell them,' I said to Danny, but that just made them think there was something to tell when there was nothing to tell. Not when we split up, that is. The name of that fourth occupant – the stranger's name I didn't recognise, the woman who isn't me and who was with my children when they died – suggests there was something to tell at a later date, something John and Lily knew, and kept from me. He had been seeing her for a while, apparently, and she was sometimes at his on the weekends when they stayed with him, but neither of them mentioned her and nor did Dan. 'Lily felt sorry for you,' her friend Saskia told me. 'She thought you were lonely.'

The night before the accident John asked me to make sponge pudding. Now I think about it, I wonder if he was trying to make me feel better about the spa visit. He knew I was angry with their dad, knew I would be left behind. Knew too that a fourth occupant would be going with them.

'If you've got money for custard I'll make it,' I said and I span off into a rant about not having any money, about having to empty the coppers jar to buy bread and toilet roll.

The driver lost control of the vehicle and the car smashed into the central reservation, killing all four occupants.

Their deaths expose me. I am raw. My body – this body which housed them and fed them – is an open wound. I am like a burn victim whose skin is re-scorched with every touch, and when I tell others I incinerate them, too. I hurt everyone and I hurt everywhere. The writing stops the hurt because inside the writing I am with my children.

I write it all down. I write about sponge pudding and custard and my children live again There is a hole where they were and words rush to fill it.

§

A SCRATCHING AT the door. It is the dog and it is day. At first I don't know where I am and then I hear a train's brakes wheezing as it creeps into the station from its sidings. I am touched by the modesty of this waiting train, its modesty and its capability. Empty carriages, freshly cleaned, seats upholstered in yellow and black, waiting to hold people and transport them. Take them somewhere they want to go.

Then the sound of Marcel crying and Rob's murmur as he moves around with him in the room below. The clock is still ticking but in daylight I find it, tucked behind some books on a shelf.

Downstairs, I slip it inside my bag. I will steal time and I will cheat it. I will rewind the hours until the moment when I am saying 'goodbye, have fun' to John and Lily and I won't let them go.

Rob is in the kitchen, sitting at the table in his dressing gown, typing fast on his laptop.

'I'll get dressed,' he says, getting up and snapping his computer shut. 'You too, Monsieur, come on.'

He tucks his laptop under one arm and heaves Marcel out of his highchair. His moccasin slippers shuffle-slap on the tiles as he leaves, taking Marcel and his laptop with him. I put away the breakfast things away and wipe down surfaces and then I follow them upstairs. I can hear Marcel playing in his parents' bedroom and I can hear the tapping of Rob's fingers on the keyboard. I knock on the door.

'Yes?'

Rob is still in his dressing gown, lying on top of his bed against the embroidered pillows, typing. Marcel is sitting in the travel cot playing with his mother's necklaces. When he sees me, he pulls himself to standing, holding onto the mesh walls of his cage.

'I could take Marcel to the park if you're working?'

'Oh, no Bobbi it's alright, thank you,' Rob says, laying his laptop aside and getting up from the bed.

'I'd like to,' I say.

'It's just that Nikki will be back soon,' Rob says.

He scruffs up his hair. I'm not sure he's telling the truth.

'I thought she was in London?'

'She's on her way – she just texted.'

Marcel makes a noise, whooping as he tosses one of the Indian necklaces out of the travel cot.

'Do you think you're ok to be on your own? Is there's someone who'll look after you?' Rob asks.

'I'm not on my own,' I say. 'I'm here with you.'

'Good, Bobbi. That's good.'

He gathers up his laptop and straightens the bedclothes.

'You're welcome to stay and talk,' he says.

'Oh no,' I say. 'I can see you're busy.'

I go back downstairs, put on my strappy sandals and let myself out of the house.

On my way home, I buy fags from Sameer.

'Not a good habit,' he tells me. 'Custard is better.'

I want to tell him that gossiping about people isn't a good habit either, but I don't say anything, just hand him my money and leave. Fox's van is parked at the end of the street. I hold out my door key and drag it along the side panel of the van as I walk past, scoring an uneven silver line in the metal. It is such a pleasurable sensation I turn around and retrace my steps, swapping my key into my nearside hand and scraping another jagged line along the bodywork.

At home, I sit in my bedroom window blowing smoke signals, waiting for Fox to see the message I have left for him. I sit there for most of the day before I spot him turning the corner at the end of the road. He is wearing a jacket and tie. He glances at the van as he approaches Sameer's shop and I see him pause and study the scratch, see his face twist into a frown. I duck out of sight as he looks around, as if the culprit might be nearby. Little Legs pads over to see what I am doing, crouched on the floor under the window.

'Shh,' I tell him.

He looks at me with sad eyes and settles down next to me, resting his chin on his paws. The shop bell rings. Fox will be telling Sameer about the vandals who have scratched his van. Sameer will tell him that only last year hooligans set light to the clubhouse on the bowling green.

I get up from the bedroom floor and go into the bathroom to wash my hands and face, brush my teeth. I count to a hundred before letting myself out of the flat.

Before I knock I try some of the breathing exercises recommended by bereavement websites. When Fox opens the door he is still wearing his jacket.

'I'm glad you came,' he says.

I can't help panting – the exercises don't help. He takes my hands and pulls me gently over the threshold. My breath comes in short, jagged bursts as I pull off his clothes. We fall awkwardly to the floor and I thrash my legs and arms against his body, against the walls and stairs and banisters of his new house.

Afterwards, he tells me he understands.

'Understand what?'

'Why you didn't say.'

Do you understand that I hallucinate my children, I want to ask? Understand that I conjure them next to me on the sofa with their phones? Understand that Lily's blouse, John's duvet are relics I hold to my face so I can breathe their smell? Understand that when I trace the outline of my tattoo with my fingertips I am remembering her doing the same? She will never have a tattoo of her own and nor will John. No-one will ever ink their skin because their skin has become ash that floats in the air.

Fox's fingers are soft but his movements are too gentle. What I need is something hard and sharp to pierce me, to score across me and cut me open. I put my clothes back on.

'Want me to come with you?' he asks, and when I say no he wishes me a safe journey across the road. He watches me tap in the door code to my building, but I don't turn and wave. I let myself into the flat, whistling quietly, waiting for John or Lily to answer with their own whistle, but their rooms are empty and there is silence apart from the clicking of Little Legs's claws as he comes to greet me.

§

I WATCH THE 24-hour news channel for twenty-four hours. Nikki's interview in front of the Scotland Yard sign plays over and over, but there is no longer a sign that reads 'live'.

'Hey!' I yell to the kids. 'The woman I work for is on TV!'

Nikki talks about a letter that one of the women was able to smuggle out.

'What did the letter say?' her interviewer asks.

'She accuses her captors of making her a non-person,' Nikki says. 'She was locked in a room and not allowed out. She refers to herself as an outline of a person.'

'Jon! Lils! The woman I work for is on the telly!'

The springs of John's mattress squeak and his bedroom door clicks open. He pads into the room and cosies up next to me, wrapped in his duvet.

'Hello my beauty!'

Then Lily emerges, too.

'Why are you being all mental?' she says, dropping onto the sofa.

John lifts my hand, placing my arm around his shoulders. Little Legs jumps off my lap and all three of us chorus 'No, Little Legs, come back!' and pat our laps to show him he is welcome. He stands in front of us, staring, and in the end Lily has to snatch him up and wedge him in between us. Meanwhile, on the television, Nikki's hair blows in front of her face and she is wearing the same clothes she wore yesterday and she is saying the same things she said yesterday, about non-people and outlines of people.

'This is the woman I work for,' I tell my children.

Nikki is talking about modern-day slaves.

'I thought slavery was abolished,' says John. 'William Wilberforce.'

'Neek' says his sister, and she tells him his duvet stinks.

'How can you stand it like that?' I ask him.

'I like the smell,' he says.

'Not the smell, I'm not talking about the smell,' I say. 'I'm talking about the bunching up.'

The duvet is lumpy and folded in on itself inside its cover. Parts of it are plump and full and other bits are like an empty sack. Like a non-duvet. Like the outline of a duvet. Sometimes, I find my own duvet like it and I have to take the cover off and re-stuff it.

I watch the news for hours and when I eventually switch off the television I can't sleep. The ticking of the clock I took from Nikki and Rob's is too loud. I tiptoe into Lily's room and hide it in her bed.

'What are you doing?' she whispers as I lift up the corner of her duvet.

'Shh. Clock's too loud,' I say, and I give the sole of her foot a little stroke. She pulls her foot away, annoyed, drawing her knees up into foetal position.

I return to my own room, but I can still hear the clock ticking.

§

MINUTES TURN INTO hours turn into days and then it is time for me to look after Marcel again. When Nikki answers the door it is a shock to see her in the flesh because I have become so used to seeing her on television. Instead of her neat skirt suit she is wearing loose trousers in a floppy material and a soft crew-necked jumper.

'Come in!' she says. 'Come in!'

She seems surprised to see me. I wipe my feet on the 'Enter' doormat.

'Weren't you expecting me?' I ask.

'We didn't know . . .' Nikki says.

She grimaces briefly and whispers something I can't hear.

'We're having coffee,' she says, recovering herself. 'Come downstairs.'

In the kitchen, Marcel is sitting on Rob's lap.

'Look who's here!' Nikki says.

She hands me a mug of coffee and we sip our drinks, oddly polite, as if we don't know one another.

'Rob told me . . . about your children,' Nikki says at last, and she flicks her hair.

'I tried to text you,' she says. 'But I just didn't know what to say.'

I tell them about my children. I tell them about visiting the crash site. I tell them about Lily's friends decorating her coffin and I tell them how John's teacher cried at his funeral.

At some point Rob must have left for work because when I finish telling my story he is no longer in the room. The old-fashioned clock on the wall ticks its steady tick and for once Pinch lies still, twitching in his sleep.

'Is it Me-Sign today?' I ask, and Nikki tells me there's no need for me to go.

'Oh, I want to,' I say.

'Are you sure?' she asks, and when I say yes she tells me she will come too.

'You shouldn't be alone,' she says.

'I won't be alone, I'll be with Marcel.'

She goes to the sink and splashes her face with water, then dabs it dry with a tea towel. She is owed time off from work so she will spend the morning with Marcel and me. Her face makes its strange contortion again.

'I'm so sorry, Bobbi.'

'What for?'

'I just feel so guilty, when you – when your . . .'

A sob makes her catch her breath and she apologises, lifts Marcel quickly out of his highchair and hurries out of the room. I sit at the kitchen table listening to the tick of the clock and the train announcements.

When Nikki returns she is calm and her her face is made up with kohl eye liner, mascara and a dusting of fine powder.

'Sorry,' she says. 'My hormones are all over the place.'

We go upstairs to get Marcel dressed, but it is Nikki who holds him and chooses his clothes. I have to look on like someone watching a play.

'There's another baby I look after . . .' I say. 'A little girl. We could take her with us, test-drive the new buggy?'

Nikki likes the idea so I phone Kim and we put Marcel

in the double buggy and wheel him down the hill to collect Jade. Nikki is pleased with the way the new buggy glides and the way its wheels turn. I walk alongside not knowing what to do with my hands.

We meet Kim outside the community centre.

'So it's some kind of music class you're taking her to, yeah?' she asks, handing me Jade.

While Nikki explains what happens in the Me-Sign session, I introduce Jade and Marcel. Jade stares at Marcel who bounces impatiently up and down in his smart buggy.

'Look, Marcel, Jade's going to sit next to you,' I say, and I sing 'Daisy, Daisy, give me your answer do' while I strap her in.

'It won't be a stylish marriage! I can't afford a carriage!'

'Cracks me up, she does,' says Kim.

Nikki suggests Kim comes with us.

'Nah, you're alright,' Kim says. 'Jade will have a good time though.'

We say goodbye and wheel the new buggy across town to the church hall where the signing instructor is pleased to see Nikki and kisses her when she learns she is pregnant. I ask her what she thinks of Daisy for a name if it's a girl, but she gives me an odd look and tells Nikki once more how nice it is to see her. Then she claps her hands to begin the session.

Nikki and I sit next to each other in the circle with Marcel on her lap and Jade on mine. As usual we start with 'Who's Me-Signing?' and the singing of each child's name. The instructor makes a fist with one hand and opens it then closes it and opens it again, making a 'spark' gesture with her fingers for Jade's name.

'Have we got Marc-el?' she sings, and we all make the letter

'M' and sing Marcel's name while he stares around the circle of women and babies. During the break Nikki spends the time talking with the instructor. I see the instructor introduce her to Ama. I wag Jade's little hand at Marcel, but he looks straight through me, as if he doesn't recognise me.

When we gather for the second half of the session, Nikki sits next to Ama on the other side of the circle from Jade and me. The instructor pulls the bird puppet onto her arm and whirls around with a 'Birdy says wel-come!' loud enough to make Jade jump. Jade is mesmerised by Birdy's bobbing eyes and reaches out for Birdy when the instructor brings it near her. The woman darts the bird away and makes a beak with her free hand.

'Bird-y,' she says to Jade, opening and shutting her finger-beak. 'Bird-y.'

She hovers the bird puppet in front of Jade, dancing it in the air and opening and shutting her finger-beak

'Bird-y! Bird-y!'

Jade raises her hand and pinces her tiny fingers together in a beak shape and there is an audible gasp from the mothers gathered in the circle. The instructor glances quickly around to make sure everyone has seen what is happening.

'Bird-y, Jade! What is it?'

Jade opens and closes her little finger-beak and a kind of creepy magic steals over the room, as if we have received a communication from The Other Side.

The instructor is triumphant.

'Wasn't that wonderful?' she whispers, her eyes as wide as the puppet's.

At the end of the session Nikki tells Jade what a clever girl she is and several of the other mothers come over to me to re-live the moment when she spoke to us in Birdy's sign language. Nikki and I pack our children into the new buggy and make our way home, stopping off at the playground with Ama and Jasmine. We sit on the edge of the sandpit and Nikki buries her feet, wriggling her toes for Marcel to pinch. She takes some bubble mixture out of her bag and blows bubbles that shimmer and pop in the air. Marcel rocks up and down on his bottom, reaching up to try and touch them.

I take Jade over to the grass under a tree where a girl of about six years old is practising cartwheels. The ends of her hair meet the blades of grass as she turns herself upside down. I whisper to Jade that one day she will be able to turn cartwheels like that big girl. We will visit parks and beaches, I tell her, and we could even go on holiday. We'll get fish and chips and eat them with tiny cardboard forks, I tell her. When you're a big girl you'll be able to do cartwheels and when you're a young woman we could get matching tattoos. You will ask me what your mum was like and I will say I'm your mum, sweetheart, and you will say you know what I mean, my real mum. Am I not real, then? I will ask and I will let you pinch me to test if I am real and to see if I can feel pain. I can feel pain. That means I am real.

§

THE NEXT TIME I arrive for my Marcel shift, instead of going downstairs to the kitchen, Nikki invites me into the living room.

'Is Marcel asleep?' I ask.

There is no sign of him and his buggy has gone from the hallway.

'No, Rob's taken him.'

She looks a bit awkward, shifts uneasily from one foot to the other. Here it comes. I knew this was coming.

'You look well, I tell her. 'You're blooming!'

'Fat, you mean!' she says, drawing her elegant cardigan around her.

'The thing is, Bobbi . . .' Nikki hugs herself, wraps her cardigan even tighter. 'The thing is, what with me on maternity and Rob just around the corner, we're both here for Marcel a bit more now and we're not sure we need anyone else – at least not until the baby's here.'

There is a wages envelope propped up on the old-fashioned writing desk. Nikki sees me spot it and picks it up, hands it to me.

'There's two months wages in there.'

'Two months?'

'Oh, this is hard! You've been wonderful with him, Bobbi, we're so grateful but . . . we need to be sure you're well enough.'

'Well enough?'

'Are you sure this kind of work, looking after children, is . . . helpful . . . to you, I mean? We're thinking about you, Bobbi. I hope you understand. We're so grateful to you, we really are.'

I catch the bus home. It is empty apart from me and an elderly lady sitting on one of the priority seats at the front.

The bell on Sameer's shop door is deafening.

'Can't you make it quieter?' I ask him, bad tempered.

He looks up from the newspaper article he is reading but he doesn't say anything. I snatch up a roll of bin-bags from a low shelf and slap them onto the counter.

§

IT TAKES ME a day and a night to clear John's room. Little Legs helps me, following me around like a fat brown shadow. I work efficiently, without stopping, without sleeping. The sounds I make are ones I made when I first learned of the crash, similar to the noise I made during childbirth – a groaning that embarrassed me with its animal-ness. I am not embarrassed now. Now I let out my animal noise. The world is asleep, anyway, no-one can hear me. When morning comes and Sameer's shutter rattles up, the sounds of birds and traffic take over.

Twelve years have been compressed into twenty-four hours and all that is left are marks on the walls where posters have been and where my boy practised keepy-uppies with balled up socks. I leave his space encyclopaedia and his Most Improved Player trophy on the empty shelves. People warned me not to let their bedrooms become a shrine. Let them warn.

I dismantle the bed his father and I assembled, piling up the pieces of its frame like firewood. His mattress was expensive, made from memory foam invented by Nasa. I lie on it and idly roam the internet on his iPad, my fingers scrolling where his once did – my fingerprints gradually rubbing out his. John and Lily were always on Facebook and Instagram, always Snapchatting their friends. I haven't deleted their accounts so their digital presence outlives them. I saw a post on Lily's timeline about a child who inherited another child's heart in a transplant operation. The dead child's mother was able to listen to her own baby's heartbeat and there was a video of her weeping. I liked that post so the person who shared it – a Facebook friend of Lily's – will receive a notification that Lily liked it and so she lives on, like the dead child's heart beating in another child's chest.

When I am done, I go across the road to ask Fox if he would like to come up to my flat.

'Only if you want me to,' he says.

'I want you to.'

We cross back over the road together and Fox watches as I key in the door code. We walk up the stairs, one behind the other, and I let him in. Little Legs inspects the visitor and follows us into John's room.

'Footballer, was he?' Fox asks, standing in the doorway.

'Yes.'

Light from the bare bulb bounces off the Most Improved Player.

'Who did he support?'

'Norwich.'

'Canary boy.'

'His dad's team – and his grandad's.'

Fox's eyes are very blue – more blue than normal. They are like a swimming pool. He has seen the biro marks on the doorframe:

John 08.07.12
John 20.04.11
John 29.07.10
John 01.01.10
John 04.09.09
John 24.12.08

'And your girl?'

'Not a footballer.'

Together, we lift the mattress down the stairs. It is light and easily handled. We prop it against the wall outside my building with a note on it. It will be gone by morning. As we are carrying the bin bags down the stairs, the woman across the landing opens her door. Seeing me, seeing the bags, she shuts it again.

Fox parks his van outside my building.

'Seen this?' he asks, showing me the scratches along the whole of one side panel.

'Terrible,' I say, but like the bowling green clubhouse, I can't feel the terribleness, I can only say it. Scratch things, burn things, they're only things. I think these thoughts, but I don't say them out loud.

'It's only a scratch,' he says, and we load the bin bags.

He tells me he will take John's things to a charity shop in a different town so I am less likely to spot a boy wearing his clothes.

He shuts the driver door and starts up the engine.

I remove the bundle of takeaway leaflets he has used to wedge the door open and I go back upstairs where Lily is waiting for me. I knew she would be.

'Why didn't you let him take this lot?' she says, leaning against the wall outside her bedroom, picking at the paintwork. She gives the doll's house a kick.

'Lily,' I say. 'Not now.'

§

THE AFTERNOONS ARE the worst. I can't be sure if the sounds I hear from the school playground at lunchtime are real or in my head. When children pass underneath my window on their way home from school, I find myself waiting for mine. Sometimes I smoke a cigarette, but mostly I try to sleep. When I wake up I find myself thinking about what to feed John for his dinner. Then I remember the dead don't need feeding.

I am hungry all the time. Fox finds it comical that I am so ravenous. He cooks up nutritious curries and stews and broths and I hang around the bubbling saucepans waiting to be fed. It's healthy I have these cravings, he tells me – it proves I am alive. He interprets this appetite of mine as my claim on the world, but really it's because I feel empty. The food I want is food I made for my children – I make sponge pudding and custard and I cut jam sandwiches on white bread into triangles. I buy packets of salt and vinegar crisps, the flavour John preferred, and I chew gum like Lily used to. My fridge is stocked with yoghurts and cream cheese, my cupboards are full of custard. I have cravings like someone who is pregnant, but I'm not pregnant, I am the opposite, bleeding heavily and losing weight. Everything passes straight through me. On some days I am eating and shitting and bleeding so much that I can't go anywhere, I have to stay where I am.

'There's nothing of you,' Fox says. 'You'll disappear if you're not careful.'

I like the thought of disappearing. At night, I lie with my arms by my sides, pretending to be dead, then I get up and go into the bathroom where I stand naked on Mum's scales. As the needle quivers I think of her and how much she weighs now. She weighs heavily on my mind and yet in terms of matter, she barely matters. What remains? Only her remains. An armchair in someone else's house.

Autumn turns into winter and Fox tells me I need pampering.

'A massage or a makeover,' he says. 'Or a haircut?'

'What's wrong with my hair?' I ask and he laughs and tells me nothing's wrong with it.

He wants to take me to London to see the Christmas lights. There is still a month to go but the city is festive and he wants to buy me presents. I make him walk past Marcel's house on our way to the station. A woman in a headscarf is manoeuvring the new double buggy down the front steps.

'Ama?'

She turns to face me.

'Bobbi!'

Fox helps her with the buggy. Jasmine and Marcel are inside, bundled up in warm jackets and wellington boots.

'Hello, Marcel!'

He shrinks away from me, hiding his face against the back of the buggy.

'You're looking after him today?' I ask Ama.

She nods and a sound of rushing fills my ears. Jasmine kicks her feet, reaching out to me. I crouch next to the buggy and take her hand in mine.

'I have him on the days his father is writing,' Ama says.

She is taking Jasmine and Marcel to the park. They won't stay long, she says, it's too cold.

'Your English is very good now,' I tell her and she smiles and thanks me, tells me she has been having lessons.

'Is that a train?' I ask Fox.

The rushing sound in my ears is very loud. Ama's hands flutter to her headscarf and when she unpins it a flock of birds fly out. They gather in a cloud and dart and swoop around us, their wings shushing, their clawed feet tangling my hair and catching my clothes as they rise into the air. I am almost lifted up with them.

'Help,' I say, but the others can't hear me. Ama is already moving along the pavement, wheeling the double buggy and Fox's mouth is moving. He is speaking but I can't hear him. The birds have gone but I am drifting upwards, a light fizzy feeling in my chest. Fox takes my hand and then we too are walking. I can feel the pavement under my feet and we are heading towards the station where he asks me what snacks I want for the train.

In Oxford Street we walk up and down watching other people shopping. There is a fever in them that can only be soothed by buying buying buying. Mine is a fever that cannot be calmed – I only want what I cannot have.

We pass a place that sells expensive watches and bracelets. It is decorated with cascades of white crystal lights – great sculptural columns that divide the shop's interior like stalactites and stalagmites. I unhook my arm from Fox's and stand in the glow of the shop's entrance.

'Do you want to go in?' Fox asks.

If I speak it will break the chemistry of the moment. The

shop's shine has transported me to a place I both know and don't know. It is a place from my past, a moment, but I'm not sure which one. I think it has something to do with a set of plastic jewellery we gave Lily for her birthday or Christmas one year. The memory is so precious, so delicious that I can almost taste it.

'Do you want to go in?' Fox asks once more.

It is the light I can taste. Is that possible? He is manoeuvring me inside the shop, but I am afraid his words and our movement will splinter the fragile glass of memory. I walk away from the shop and then quickly retrace my steps. Fox is wrong-footed, he doesn't understand.

'Bobbi,' he says. 'What's the matter?'

I am trying to recreate the moment in which I saw the glitter of a plastic jewellery set through my daughter's eyes, which in turn is a memory inside the moment my girl's delight and my own girlish delight was captured, Russian doll-like, inside these sparkling shop lights. Fox follows me while I chase something shiny and rainbowish through the tunnels of my mind, trying to catch it, trying to capture the anticipation of Lily's pleasure in the phoney diamante necklace, then her actual delight in it when she unwrapped her present and I put it around her tender neck.

'Catch her,' I whisper, snatching at the memory. It is impossible, though. I smack my lips, trying to get the taste back, but it is gone.

I can't sleep. I hear my children calling. I unpeel myself from Fox and get out of bed, pull aside the curtain and peer across the road. My bedroom window opposite is dark, but I can hear Lily calling for me. I scan the pavements below – maybe she's locked out. Maybe she is sheltering in the porch to our building and shouting up at my bedroom window. I put on my clothes and let myself out, crossing back over the road.

There is no-one home. I get into my own bed and lie staring at the ceiling until I hear the front door click and Lily creeping in, removing her Doc Martens.

'I heard you calling,' I say, and my voice makes her jump.

'I didn't call,' she says.

She drifts into her bedroom and shuts the door.

I can't find John. He isn't on the sofa and he isn't in his bed.

§

ANDY ORGANISES A Christmas party for the young people. Keji wears a puffed sleeve satin dress and an elaborately pleated headscarf in the same material. The others wear their uniform of tracksuit bottoms and trainers.

'Is there anything to drink?' Kim asks.

'There's no alcohol, but we've got a very special guest,' Andy says.

There is no sign of Connor and when I ask Kim where he is she shrugs and tells me she's not his keeper is she. Something in her manner stops me asking her if I can hold Jade. She seems prickly, defensive. I overhear her telling the others how she and Connor broke into a car.

'There were loads of presents in the back and one of them looked like it could be a PlayStation,' she says. 'Turns out it wasn't a PlayStation, it was kitchen shit. What fucker gives someone a saucepan for Christmas?'

Keji thinks a saucepan is a good present. Kim tells her Connor's giving it to his mum.

Andy announces the arrival of the mystery guest and asks everyone to bring their chairs into a circle. He leaves the room and returns with a lanky Father Christmas.

'Look who it is, everyone!'

'Ho ho ho,' says Father Christmas.

He carries a bin bag of presents and has a love bite on his neck.

'Do we have to sit on your lap?' Nat asks.

'Yeah, come and sit on my lap and I'll give you one,' says Santa.

He slaps his knees, but no-one takes up his offer. Nat tries to persuade JD to go up, but he has both hands deep in a bowl of cheesey puffs and is working his way through the feast Andy and I laid out on one of the tables.

'Come on, JD! Santa might give you a present if you've been a good boy,' Nat tells him but her child refuses to go near Father Christmas, running behind the chairs with fistfuls of crisps.

'Maybe if you take off the beard,' Andy suggests and Connor drops the ratty cotton wool beard onto the floor.

'Look, it's only Connor,' Nat says to JD, and she takes him by the hand and leads him to stand in front of Connor who digs inside his bin bag for a present. JD tears off the wrapping paper and kisses the toy car inside the parcel.

He goes around the circle showing it to everyone then drives it along every available surface, brum-brumming it along windowsills and the edges of chairs and tables.

'It's what Christmas is all about, isn't it?' Andy whispers.

'Who's next?' Connor says, and without needing any further invitation, Nat sits on his lap.

'Have you been a good girl?' Connor asks.

'I've been a very bad girl,' Nat says.

'How about a kiss for Father Christmas?'

'You do, Connor, and I'll fucking kill you,' Kim says.

But it is too late, Nat has her eyes closed and she and Connor are kissing. Kim is out of her seat, the chair she was sitting on skids from underneath her, and she thrusts Jade into my arms. Before anyone can stop her, she has pulled Nat off Santa's lap and onto the floor where she sits on top of her, punching her in the head and snatching at her hair.

'Bitch!'

Nat screams and Andy rushes to protect her while Connor sits smirking in his Father Christmas outfit. Kim is standing now, screaming abuse and kicking Nat while Andy tries to contain her, his arms around her. JD stops brum brum brumming his new car to stare at his mother curled up on the floor. I grab his hand and take him outside.

'Mummy and Kim had an argument,' I tell him. 'They're just sorting things out.'

He shivers as we shelter in the doorway looking for Santa's reindeer, a sleety rain blowing in our faces, and then Andy comes to tell us the party is over.

I get home and write all about the young people and their Christmas party. Writing is a way of keeping things and a way of leaving something behind. I can't do anything without writing. It all gets written down. At night, when I catch my reflection in the dark kitchen window, there is something of Lily in the slope of my neck, in the hunch of my shoulders. If I squint at the figure I can pretend it is her, sitting at the table doing her homework.

Fox proposes day trips and evening entertainments, but all I want to do is write. I stay at his for Christmas and he asks me to move in with him. He tells me he wants to look after me.

'Who says I need looking after?' I say.

'Everyone needs looking after.'

All I want to do is write.

'When can I read your writing?' he asks, and I tell him there is more to be written.

I write everywhere. I write in Lily's old diary, I write in the air, like people do when they signal to a waiter for the bill in a busy restaurant. I even write during sex – Fox's penis is as shapely as a quill and when he is inside me I move my hips to make words against the bed sheets.

'Don't go,' he says, when I am ready to cross the road back to mine. 'I like having you here.'

'Little Legs needs me,' I tell him.

What I don't tell him is that the children have been gone a long time and I am waiting for them to come back. If I am elsewhere they won't know where to find me.

§

NEITHER KIM NOR Connor are at the first Life Skills session after the Christmas break. When I am helping Andy stack the chairs, I ask if he has heard from them.

'I doubt we'll see much more of Kim or Connor,' he says. 'It's a shame.'

He rests one hand on the chair at the top of our pile and says he will tell me something in confidence.

'Kim and Jade have been moved to a safe house.'

'A safe house?'

'There was an incident... It's not the first time.'

'Where are they?' I ask. 'I'd like to help if I can.'

'That's kind, Bobbi, but I'm afraid I can't tell you where they're staying. Jade was injured so it's a safeguarding issue.'

The room shimmers, the pile of chairs seems precarious, as if it might topple. Andy places his hand on mine.

'I'm Sorry, Bobbi, I know you're fond of them.'

'Is Jade alright?'

'She is now.'

I try phoning Kim, but her number is no longer recognised. Then one day I am at the park with Little Legs and I receive a text from an unknown number.

can u call me pls urgent

I sit on a bench under dripping trees to ring the number. The park is empty. In a few hours its paths will be criss-crossed with parents collecting their children from school, and later still with people making their way home from work. For now, though, it is just Little Legs and me.

'Bobbi, thank fuck.'

'Kim? Where are you?'

'Not allowed to say. Bournemouth.'

'How's Jade?'

'Not good, not good. She's got a fucking great bruise on her face.'

'What happened?'

'Connor's what happened.'

A breeze shivers through the trees. Kim tells me she and Connor had a fight and she was holding Jade when Connor tried to hit her. I feel faint, lean over to put my head between my knees. I concentrate on the feeling of the bench's moisture seeping through my clothes. Little Legs hobbles over to sniff my hair.

'Bobbi? Are you still there?'

'I'm still here, yes.'

'They're not letting me see him.'

'If he's violent, Kim, it's best to stay out of his way.'

'That's what everyone says, but it's not as easy as that, is it.'

'But if he's been violent and Jade's been hurt --'

'I 'ain't allowed to speak to anyone. It's like prison. I had to give them my other phone in case he tries to contact me.'

'How's Jade?'

'Apart from her fucking face, you mean?'

I hear a seagull's cry at the other end of the line.

'If I see him or speak to him they'll take her off me, Bobbi.'

'They're trying to help.'

'Bunch of cunts.'

She tells me that unless she can separate from Connor, Jade will be emergency fostered.

'Oh, Kim, you don't want that, do you.'

'Course I don't, but it's not like he's a paedo.'

'But if he's got a history of violence . . .'

'Bobbi, you're starting to sound like one of them.'

The phone line crackles as she moves around at the other end.

'Listen, I gotta go now but meet me, yeah? Social's bringing me in for an appointment next week.'

'I don't want to get you into trouble,' I say.

'Fuck that,' she says.

§

THE CLOCKS SPRING forward so I have one less hour to wait until I see Jade. I sit in bed with Nikki and Rob's clock in my hands, watching hours and minutes tick past.

Finally, it is time. I have arranged to meet Kim in a café. It is empty when I get there, apart from an old man who sits with the waitress at a table in one corner. They look up when I slam the café door and the waitress gets up and goes into a kitchen at the back. The old man spreads out his newspaper, smoothing its pages. The waitress brings him a cup of tea and comes over to me, pen poised over a tiny notebook.

'What can I get you?'

Star shaped notices in fluorescent coloured card stuck on the windows announce egg & chips and meal deals for pensioners.

'I'm waiting for someone,' I say.

The waitress nods and retreats once more to the kitchen, then the door bangs and Kim backs into the cafe with Jade in a buggy.

'She's in a buggy now!' I say, as we angle the pushchair through the door one manoeuvre at a time.

Jade's little body shunts from side to side.

'Place I'm in isn't big enough for a pram,' Kim says.

She looks tired. Her hair is greasy and hangs lank around her pale face.

'I see you've still got your pretty unicorn cushion though, Jade!'

'Get her out if you like.'

I lift Jade out of her buggy and sit her on my lap. She wears her pink headband with the pink flower on it.

'Her hair's grown,' I say.

'I can't do nothing with it. It's got a mind of its own.'

Kim reaches across the table to pull aside the stretchy pink headband.

'Her bruise is going down – you can hardly see it now.'

A brownish yellow mark stains the pale skin at Jade's temple. Kim covers it with the headband once more and the waitress comes over.

'Bacon butty,' Kim says, without looking at her.

'And I'll have a round of toast, please.'

The waitress nods, writes.

'Any drinks?'

I order tea and Kim asks for a Coke. The waitress writes down our order and adds a decisive full stop before pocketing her pad and pen.

'So how have you been?' I ask, once the waitress has left.

'As well as can be expected.'

'And Connor? Have you had any contact?'

'Not since the night he smacked her,' Kim says. I 'ain't seen anyone since that night. It's just been me and her. She's my rock.'

She reaches across to take her daughter's hand.

'They're going to take her away.' Kim says, adjusting Jade's headband once more.

'Hopefully it won't come to that.'

'You don't know what they're like, Bobbi. They'll take her off me.'

I have the sensation of Jade lifting out of my arms, as if she might float up into the air and out of the café window.

'Love her to bits, but I might not be the best parent for her.'

'That doesn't sound like you speaking.'

'What are you talking about? Who else is it?'

The waitress arrives with our order. She sets the can of Coke down noisily on the table in front of Kim, places a mug of tea in front of me.

'They're saying I got to stop seeing Connor. Social are telling me there's got to be no contact, but he's her dad!'

She is about to say something else but stops herself.

'Smashed that doll, didn't I,' she says.

'What doll?'

'That one I made of Connor at Life Skills. Kept the one I made of her though.'

She peels a crust off my toast and puts it in Jade's hand, closing her little fingers around it. Jade wags it uselessly in front of her face and Kim laughs.

'Loves her food,' she says. 'Bread's her favourite.'

'Are you weaning her, then?'

'Weaning, yes.'

She takes a sip of Coke. 'Social worker said you would be a good person to come to the hearing. I need someone with me.'

'I'll come. I'm here for you.'

'Do you reckon he'll be there?'

'Who?'

'Connor. I don't reckon he will. He don't care about us, he only cares about himself.'

'That's probably true.'

'Do you think he'll turn up? He most probably won't turn up, will he?'

I try to understand what the hearing will determine, but Kim is focussed on the issue of whether Connor will be there and repeats her mantra about not being the best parent for her daughter. Then she says it is time for her to leave.

'Man about a dog,' she says.

She tips back her head to drain her can, then holds out her arms for Jade. I pay for our drinks and we shunt our way awkwardly out of the café while the waitress stands behind her counter watching us.

'Nice of someone to help,' Kim says loudly, as she struggles with the door, and once we are outside on the pavement she tells me 'that was my auntie.'

'Who? The waitress?'

'My mum's sister, yeah. They don't speak. I don't have nothing to do with Mum's side of the family.'

She is amused by how surprised I am.

'See the old geezer reading the paper?' she says, and I glance through the café window where the man in the corner has looked up from his newspaper and is staring at us. 'That's my grandad.'

After Kim and I have parted, I wander around the shops.

'What kind of look are you after?' asks a young sales assistant at a make-up counter. 'A natural kind of look?'

'Something natural, yes,' I tell her.

She invites me to take a seat and talks me through various products from the 'Barely There' range, briskly rubbing foundation onto the back of her hand and dabbing it onto my cheeks. Her own make-up is heavy like a mask and her face hovers close to mine as she works. I close my eyes and pretend she is Lily as she dusts my nose, chin and forehead with powder and shines my lips. I want to feel her fingers on my face forever.

Afterwards, I wander into a clothes shop in my natural make-up, picking up items and holding them next to my body, stretching the sleeves along my arms and imagining how they would look on Lily, wondering if she would have chosen them for herself, wondering if she would have made me take them back to the shop if I had bought them for her. I pick up a pair of shoes and one of the young women comes over and asks if I would like to try them on. I ask her for Lily's size, knowing they won't fit, but even so I sit on the low stool provided and squeeze my toes inside them. The assistant watches me. She is probably only Lily's age – or the age Lily would be now. She might even be the same school year as Lily. They might have been at the same school.

'I'll take them, they're perfect,' I tell her.

'Really?'

She fiddles nervously with her jewellery – a word I can't read in gold letters on a chain around her neck. Her name, perhaps.

'They're not for me,' I tell her and the young woman looks relieved, lets go of her necklace and takes the shoes from me, putting them in their box and covering them with a thin layer of tissue paper.

I find myself in a bookshop next, in the children's section, where I am drawn to a story about a princess who has to spin gold for the king. I sit on a beanbag to read it. A brother and a sister sit next to one another on another beanbag, poring over an annual the girl holds on her lap. She traces its words with her finger as she whispers them to her brother. Their brindled heads touch as the boy leans against his sister to show her something in the book. Their mother catches me watching them and tells her children she will be 'just over there'. She points at the crime section where one or two others are killing time.

The boy's concentration reminds me of John hunched over his encyclopaedia of space. The girl is long-limbed and sits with her legs stretched out in front of her, just like Lily used to. I see traces of them everywhere. I close my eyes to experiment with not looking and I hear the boy whisper to his sister 'that lady's fallen asleep'. There is a rustle as they move off and when I open my eyes they have gone.

I take the book about straw and gold to the till.

'Do you know about the local-author event we're hosting this evening?' the bookseller asks.

She gestures at a poster and a pile of books displayed on the counter. The image on the poster and on the cover of the books shows a block of flats that looks a bit like the building I live in and a woman who doesn't look like a bit like me. The sky is red, as if it is burning.

'The author's coming here to speak about his work,' the bookseller tells me, and I turn the book over in my hands.

Rob smiles at me from the back cover. I tell the young woman I'll stay and she says there's three pounds off the price of the book if I buy a copy at the event. She turns the 'Open' and 'Closed' sign around on the shop door and I take Rob's book back to my beanbag. I recognise Nikki in a description of her bangles and bare feet on the first page. I am there too, arriving flustered and polite, wiping my feet. Rob wasn't even present the first time I came to his house so how can he know what happened?

The bookseller spreads a white table cloth on a nearby table and arranges books and bottles of wine while I read. I read and read and the reading is what I have been writing, what I have been living. I read about Marcel, about Fox, about my mother and my children, about the omelette I make, mirrors I look in, sexy underwear I wear. An odd sensation steals over me, as if I don't exist outside of the words I am reading, these words in which I have been shaped. I feel naked, my heart knocks loudly in my chest. I am having an out of body experience.

I turn the book over in my hands and study the author photograph and when I look up again a small crowd has gathered, and here comes Rob in his crumpled linen jacket, a leather satchel hanging from his shoulder, newer and smarter than the one he used to take to work. He is ushered to a seat by a slender young woman in a mannish suit. The bookseller pours wine into plastic cups. I spot Nikki standing by the door. She wears a white sheath dress which shows off her bump.

The young woman introduces Rob to the crowd and he smiles, scanning our faces.

'So, firstly, thank you for being here,' the young woman says.

'You're most welcome,' Rob says, placing his leather satchel on the floor next to his chair.

'Why don't we begin with you telling us a little bit about your book?'

Rob explains that his book is written in the first person from the point of view of a woman.

'Yes,' says the mannish young woman. 'And yet you, if you don't mind me saying so, are a man . . .'

Rob smiles at her and tells her you don't have to be a woman to write as one.

'I know women,' he says. 'I live with one.'

The wine tastes unpleasant, but the ridges on the plastic cup are a comfort. I run my thumb up and down them.

'Your wife's here, I think?' The young woman lifts herself up off her chair slightly to scan the crowd, but she doesn't see Nikki, even when she gives a modest wave from the doorway of the shop.

'A writer can only write about themselves,' Rob says. 'This book is all about me.'

'So you're saying it's autobiographical?' the young woman asks.

'I am,' Rob says.

He touches his hair with both hands, smoothing it behind his ears.

The woman asks Rob if he will read a section from his book and he says he will. He takes a copy out of his smart leather satchel and turns to a page marked with a strip of paper. The description he reads is of a woman hovering close to another woman as she works. One woman closes her eyes and wishes she could feel her fingers on her face forever. The words feel like a message, as if Rob is trying to tell me something, but what?

When he stops reading, people clap and the bookseller invites us to buy copies of his book. Rob will sign them for us, she says. The crowd breaks up with some people heading to the till and others approaching Rob's table.

I move towards the door.

'Do I exist?' I ask Nikki.

'Bobbi!'

She laughs and takes my arm.

'Want to get your book signed? Rob will be so pleased to see you.'

'How's Marcel?' I ask, but she doesn't hear me. She has my hand in hers and she is leading me through the crowd, gliding ahead of me like a ghost.

'Look who's here,' she says to Rob.

She wears a striking necklace made out of gold. It is more of a collar than a necklace, with spokes that have tiny letters on the end, spelling out the title of Rob's book. He glances at me and excuses himself to the customer whose book he has just signed. 'Sorry,' he says. 'I just have to say hello to someone . . .' The customer thanks Rob and moves off, tucking his book under her arm.

'I hope you enjoy it,' Rob calls after the customer, twisting the cap back onto his fountain pen. Then he turns to me.

'Bobbi, it's so nice to see you. Thank you for coming. How are you?'

'Who am I?'

Rob laughs. 'How are you? Are you well?'

'I don't know . . . am I?'

'I told Bobbi you'd sign her book for her,' Nikki says, lifting it out of my hands.

She places it on the table in front of Rob and he uncaps his pen. He looks up at me.

'Bobbi or Roberta?'

'What?'

'Who shall I write it to? Bobbi or Roberta?'

'You decide,' I tell him.

'Bobbi,' Nikki tells him. 'With an "i".'

He signs my book with a flourish then blows on the ink to dry it. He hands it back to me and stands, thanking me for coming. He leans across the table to kiss me on both cheeks. He kisses me first on one cheek and then on the other but the second kiss catches me by surprise and instead of his lips landing on my cheek, he kisses me on the mouth. I leave the shop in a hurry and once I am outside I start running. I run as fast as I can but I can't get away from the smell of his aftershave in my hair. I race through the streets, trying to shake off the phantom at my back, the someone who is chasing me.

I spend most of the night reading Rob's book, reading about myself and my life while Little Legs twitches in the bed next to me. When I eventually fall asleep I dream I am getting married. In my dream, Jade is helping me choose a wedding dress. We look through catalogues together. Then we are in the pages of a catalogue trying on wedding dresses. Jade is trying on dresses, turning around and around showing me how they look. As she turns she turns into Lily. Lily and I visit the place we will get married and it is the beach in one of the photographs in Nikki's hallway. The sand is soft between our toes and there are parrots in the trees. It is just me and Lily. We are on a desert island. We are getting married.

I wake up from the dream and I am desolate not to be with my dream girl. Little Legs doesn't like it when I cry. He jumps off the bed and paces around the flat weaving silently from room to room. When he can't find what he's looking for he comes back into my bedroom and stands on his hind legs, clawing at the bedclothes, driving his snout underneath the duvet, trying to lever me out of bed.

Eventually, his protests have me on my feet. I pull on some clothes and put him on his lead. We let ourselves quietly out of the flat. The sky is burning red and the rest of the world is sleeping, it seems. It's too early for street cleaners – or newsagents, even – Sameer's shutters are down. Little Legs and I pass the library and head towards the station.

I smoke a cigarette under a lamppost then tug Little Legs up the front steps where I take a hand shaped doorknocker in mine. I let go of the lead and Little Legs hops down the steps. I could knock loud enough to wake the dead, but I replace the knocker carefully without making a noise. Little Legs is waiting for me. I peer through the letterbox. The hallway is a queasy kind of dark and the double buggy stands at the bottom of the stairs. In the half-light I can see the indentation Manel's body has made in its fleecy lining. I snap the letterbox shut and from inside the house I hear Pinch bark.

The plant pots are too heavy to lift so I scrabble the soil with my bare hands. Little Legs watches me as I work fast to unpack the earth. On the other side of the door Pinch paces back and forth. I can hear the thud of his tail. I yank out the ornamental tree and chuck it into the road. Pushing the pot with my foot, it smashes down the steps. Pinch barks and inside the house a light goes on.

'Quick, Little Legs, run!

He scampers after me, trailing his lead. When we are safely around the corner I scoop up its end and we walk home singing 'Morning Has Broken' at the tops of our voices.

§

WHEN WE LET ourselves into the flat I can tell right away Lily is home because my straighteners are still hot and the vanilla perfume she wears hangs in the air.

'Lils? Is that you?'

She won't come out of her bedroom so I have to speak to her from the other side of the door. I tell her about the new shoes I bought.

'You can try them on if you like,' I tell her.

She opens the door a crack.

'Hello, sweetness.'

She is a young woman now, but she is still my sweet girl.

'Let's see the shoes,' she says.

I fetch them and pass her the box through the crack in her door.

'Are you moving in with that guy over the road?'

I take this as my cue to come into her room and sit next to her on her bed.

'No,' I say. 'I live here, with you.'

She removes tissue paper from the box, takes out one of the shoes. She loves them, I can tell.

'Wear them if you like,' I say.

I persuade her out of her room to watch television and we flick through the channels until I find a nature documentary. Lily stretches her legs across my lap, her feet hanging off the end of the sofa in the new shoes.

On the television a mother spider regurgitates prey for her babies.

'Clever mama spider,' I say.

Lily points out that perhaps she's not so clever – extra digestive enzymes she has produced in order for her to eat more prey are melting away her insides, leaving just her heart and ovaries.

'Her body becomes a highly nutritious food source for her offspring, who proceed to eat her' says the narrator.

'Come to think of it, I'm starving,' Lily says.

'What do you want? Biscuits? Pizza?'

'Both.'

The mother spider offers her body as both grave and nursery, so fetching snacks for my ghost girl is the least I can do.

Fox texts.

u ok?

I text him back.

clearing L's room

take yr time x

She lies on her bed listlessly scrolling through her phone while I go through her clothes, holding up items and asking if she remembers this skirt or that top, asking her if they still fit. She tells me how good my new shoes would look with every outfit. She wants to borrow them but I won't let her. If I deny her the shoes she will stay.

'I don't want you not to exist,' I say.

'What are you talking about?' she asks.

'I don't . . . I don't want you to not exist,' I repeat, but she isn't listening, she has turned her attention to her eyebrows, which she is plucking, complaining to anyone who will listen that she has a monobrow.

Into a bag for the charity shop goes the mirror she used to look in. Somebody else will look in it now. I keep her nail varnishes and her perfume, her coconut moisturiser. I will paint my own nails in her colours, sweeten and moisturise my own skin, even as cells shed and are replaced. I remove Post-it notes from the wall around her desk, some have rules and equations and scientific facts written on them, others have Shakespeare quotes in her childish handwriting.

Lend me a look-glass.
If that her breath will mist or stain the stone,
Why then, she lives.

She is annoyed when I try to flatten out the creases in the pencil portrait she drew of her grandmother. I want to frame it and put it on the wall, but she won't let me.

'I'll have it in my bedroom where no-one will see it apart from me,' I say, but she won't allow it.

'It's rubbish,' she says.

She tells me her feet are cold.

'Look, they're turning blue!' she says. 'What I need is a nice pair of shoes.'

'You can't have them.' I tell her. 'You can only borrow them.'

'I hate you!' she shrieks. 'You're the worst mother in the world!'

The violence of her passion floors me, but I would have this any day over her absence. She has been gone such a long time.

In the end, after days of her pestering, I let her have them and sure enough, as soon as she gets what she wants, she disappears.

§

THE DATE FOR Kim's hearing comes around. We arrange to meet outside the Family Court. Andy is with her when I arrive. When she sees me she throws down her cigarette and grinds it under her foot.

'Fucking freezing,' she says, thrusting her hands into the pockets of her padded coat.

Jade is in her buggy, swaddled in a puffer jacket against the wind that whistles up the main road.

'She's looking so grown up!' I say.

'Yeah, she's getting big,' Kim says, bouncing from one foot to the other trying to keep warm. 'Do you reckon Connor will come? I don't reckon he will. He doesn't care about us, he only cares about himself.'

We lift Jade's buggy up the steps. Inside the building a security guard ushers us one by one through a metal detector. Kim goes first and as the guard scans her body from head to toe, sweeping his baton around her ankles and around Jade's buggy, I pretend we are taking a holiday together. But instead of going through customs to board a plane, we get into a lift that takes us up to a courtroom.

'I don't reckon he'll be there,' Kim says, checking her reflection in the mirrored walls of the lift, tugging at her hoop earrings and tightening her ponytail. 'He won't even bother to show up.'

Andy glances at me and Kim catches the look he gives me.

'What?' she says, jutting out her chin at him. 'Do you know something I don't?'

'I don't know anything,' Andy says. 'All I know is that Connor is bad news.'

'I know that, don't I!' she says in a loud voice. 'You don't have to tell me. Wish I'd never set eyes on him.'

Kim's social worker ushers us into a blue carpeted room full of pale furniture. There is a coat of arms on the wall. We are shown where to sit. Kim gets Jade out of her buggy and jiggles her on her knee, but when the door opens she passes her to me. Connor walks in, accompanied by his social worker. He takes a seat on the other side of the room, as if we are relatives at a wedding and he is on the groom's side. He doesn't look at Kim but she doesn't take her eyes off him.

We are asked to stand when the judge enters through a different door. Connor hauls himself to his feet, as if a great effort is required. The judge tells us to sit and she sits herself, behind a desk on a raised podium. She explains that unless Kim can guarantee Jade's safety, her care will be handed over to a foster family. Her voice is gentle but firm when she asks Kim if she understands what is being said.

'Please answer yes or no,' she says, and Kim says 'yes'.

The judge tells us Connor is permitted to see Jade only during supervised contact hours and then we are asked to stand again while the judge leaves.

'Is that it?' I ask, and Andy tells me that it is.

Kim's social worker suggests we wait for Connor to go before we make our move.

'He ain't seeing her – no way,' Kim says loudly.

Connor grins at her as he lopes towards the door and Kim's social worker lays a hand on her arm.

'Don't let him wind you up.'

'Too late,' she shouts, and she hurdles the rows of seats to hit him and scratch him. Andy and her social worker scramble after her while I turn away, holding Jade close. I clasp Jade's head to my chest and find her soft baby hair comes off in my hands. The curls float out of my fingers like dandelion down and when I look at her she has a proper haircut and she is grown. Her arms stick out of the sleeves of her puffer jacket and her legs dangle awkwardly, her feet touching the floor.

'But you're so big!' I cry as she steps away from me. 'Look how tall you are!'

She takes my hands in hers and we skip around the courtroom. Her new big-girl hair streams out behind her like a flag.

'Look how straight and long it's grown!' I marvel. 'Did you make a bargain with the king?'

'The king, yes!' she cries.

'It's like someone else's hair,' I say.

'It is someone else's hair!' she tells me. 'I had extensions put in!'

'Like Lily wanted!'

'Who's Lily?' she asks and she laughs so prettily I can't believe she was a baby only moments ago.

'You were a baby only five minutes ago!' I say and I tell her how amazing she is, how good she is at dancing and skipping and talking.

'Are you feeling alright, Bobbi?' Andy asks.

Kim and Connor have gone and the courtroom is empty. Andy takes Jade from me and hands her to the social worker who puts her in her pushchair and wheels her into a side room where I catch a glimpse of Kim sitting at a table, her head in her hands.

Andy tells me he will give me a lift home. He takes my arm, linking mine in his on the way down in the lift to the car park. Arm in arm we must look like an old married couple and yet the truth is, Andy doesn't even know where I live, I have to tell him my address.

On the journey I ask what will happen to Jade.

'It's likely she will be removed,' he says, staring ahead into traffic.

'I could look after her.'

'It's not us who makes the decision, Bobbi.'

'Whose decision is it?'

'There are a number of agencies involved.'

I ask him if I could become her guardian. I've looked after her, she knows me. We have a relationship. I don't like the idea of her going to strangers.

'The local authority would go to a lot of trouble choosing an appropriate setting for a case like this,' Andy says, trying to reassure me.

'All the same, they're strangers – they don't know her like I know her. She's been to my home, she spent the night.'

'I think Jade will be fostered in a different part of the country,' he says, slowing the car as we approach my road.

'Is this you?' he asks.

He turns into my street and I point out my flat. He pulls up outside.

'I'm sorry, Bobbi,' he says. 'I'm just being realistic.'

I thank him for the lift and get out of the car. He leans across the passenger seat, craning forward so that his seatbelt stretches taut.

'They prefer a clean slate . . . A blank page, if you know what I mean?'

As soon as I am indoors I take out Lily's old diary and I sit down to write. The silver pencil feels heavy in my hand as I write about Jade's puffer jacket, the mirrored lift, the blue carpeted room.

It's getting late and Little Legs and I are at the park. We sit on a bench near the patch of burnt ground where the bowling green clubhouse once stood. There is no breath of wind, everything is still. A spider hangs motionless in its web. It's as if something is about to happen.

'Got a cigarette?'

It is the guy with the teardrops tattooed on his face. I offer him my packet of fags.

'Your last one.'

'Take it.'

Teardrop puts the cigarette in his mouth. I flick my lighter and its flame burns in the gathering darkness.

'Sorry – sorry to ask . . .'

I empty the contents of my purse into his cupped hands and he thanks me then limps quickly away. Little Legs follows him along the path. When I whistle, Teardrop turns around. He sees Little Legs and signals to me, pointing at the dog, as if to let me know he is there. I raise a hand and wave. Teardrop waves back. Little Legs pauses, halfway across the park, but he doesn't move. I whistle once more but he doesn't move. He is caught between us, rooted to the spot by his four silly paws. Then Teardrop whistles.

'Go on then,' I say, and my mother's dog trots after his new owner.

§

I STOP GOING to Life Skills, I stop going to the park. I stop shopping at Sameer's.

Here for you x

I stop texting Fox. Kim is back with Connor and Jade is to be handed over to foster parents for a trial period. It will become a permanent arrangement if Kim can't make the changes social workers are asking her to make.

Their taking Jade. Told u they wld

She asks if I will come with her to the family court.

'I'll come,' I tell her, 'butI don't know what I can do.'

'You can't do nothing, Bobbi, no-one can. You know what it's like to lose a daughter, though.'

A Shakespeare quote I learned at school floats into my head, something about how tender it is to give suck, but I need Lily's Post-it notes to remember it properly and I have stripped her room bare.

Kim arrives early, with Jade looking pretty in her best dress. She wears a new gold bangle Kim has bought her 'so she remembers me.'

We carry her buggy up the stairs and Kim sits on my bedroom windowsill to smoke a cigarette. She fiddles with her disposable lighter, tossing it from one hand to the other, lighter fluid bouncing inside its amber casing like nectar.

'Think you'd die if you fell out?' she asks, gesturing out of the window.

'I reckon so.'

'I reckon so an' all. Smash yourself to bits. Either that or you'd be a vegetable.'

She stares at her daughter in my arms and takes a last drag of her cigarette before tossing it out of the window.

'I need a drink,' Kim says. 'You alright with her if I go to the shop?'

'Have you got time?'

'Got to be there for twelve. What time's it now?'

Jade and I watch her out of the window. The bell on the shop door rings as she disappears inside. In half an hour we will be in the blue-carpeted room of the family court, with its raised dais and the coat of arms above the judge's chair. Kim's social worker and Andy will be there, and maybe Connor too. Jade's new foster parents will be there.

The bell rings once more and Kim comes out and crosses the road, a 350ml bottle of whisky weighing down the pocket of her coat. The judge will smell the drink on her breath and order Jade to be looked after by foster parents, for there to be phone contact only with the birth mother.

My door buzzer goes.

She will be adopted if Kim fails to convince social workers she is capable of looking after her.

'What shall we do?' I ask Jade.

The intercom buzzes again and Jade turns her head in the direction of the sound.

'Uh!' she says.

'Oh!' I say. 'Did Jade hear something?'

My phone rings in my bag and the little darling twists around in my arms.

'Uh!' she says once more.

'Is that my phone?' I ask her, and I carry her into the kitchen where my bag hangs on a chair.

'Who's calling me? Is it Jade's mummy?'

We check my phone display and I press 'decline' as the door buzzer goes again, a prolonged, insistent note this time. Outside, Kim shouts up from the pavement.

'Bobbi! Let us in!'

A small stone hits the living room window

'Your mummy's a good [illegible]

I close the curtains.

'Bobbi! What the fuck? We have to be in court at twelve!'

I can hear my neighbour's door buzzer and a conversation at the intercom. Someone lets Kim into the building and her feet slap up the stairs, her fists pound on my front door. Jade and I hide in my bedroom while her mother calls my name. A rattle of the letterbox is followed by a hissed 'what the fuck' and then silence.

I imagine her sliding to the landing floor, drinking her whisky.

'Uh!' says Jade, and Kim hears her.

'Bobbi are you in there? What the fuck's going on?'

I put my finger to my lips and then place it gently on Jade's mouth. Her lips are perfect, like the prettiest seashell on a beach. She is a mermaid, a princess. Outside my flat, Kim is talking on the phone.

'At Bobbi's – she's got Jade in her flat and she won't let me in, fucking nutjob! Come and sort it out . . . Court's at twelve . . . she's your daughter too!'

Cursing, she ends the phone call and there is a moment's silence before I hear her talking to Andy.

'I'm at Bobbi's . . . Bobbi's. Jade's inside her flat and I can't get in, there's no answer . . . I dunno, I'm worried she might have had a heart attack . . . yes, twelve o'clock.'

She thinks I'm dead on the floor and her baby uncared for, but I would never abandon Jade like that. I cough to let her know.

'Bobbi?'

The letterbox rattles again.

'I'm here,' I say. 'You go. Jade will be alright with me.'

'What are you talking about, you muppet? Let me in, I left my lighter in your bedroom.'

'They'll take her. You said so yourself.'

'I'm going to fight for her – me and Connor, we're going to get her back. If we go to court like they want, they'll foster her for a bit and then we'll get her back. Bobbi, let us in.'

'I'm not going to let them take her.'

'Nor am I!'

She bangs on the door and Jade starts to cry so I take her into the kitchen where we look in the fridge for something she might like. I show her the picture of a cow on a packet of cream cheese.

'Moo!' I say. 'Can you say "moo"?'

Jade jigs up and down on my hip making 'mm' 'mm' noises while her mother is shouting to someone about me kidnapping her kid. My neighbour across the landing has come out of her flat to complain. I unwrap a cheese triangle and Jade mushes it in her little fist, cramming it in her mouth. I stroke her hair and tell her the story about the farmer's daughter who spins straw into gold.

'Bobbi, you mad cow,' Kim yells through the letterbox. 'Your neighbour's calling the filth.'

'The daughter has to fill the room with gold by morning,' I whisper to Jade. 'So she gets a horrible little man to help her, but he demands her firstborn child unless she can guess his name.'

Outside my flat, Kim is on the phone to Connor again, telling him to stay out of sight while the police are here.

'You'll make me lose her, Bobbi!' she yells

'She's lost already,' I tell her.

'You're not the fucking judge!'

But the judge will smell the whisky on her and she will see the way she looks at Connor and Jade will be handed over.

'I can save you the pain,' I tell her, and I tell Jade about the farmer's daughter spying on the little man in the woods when he's dancing around a fire.

'What are you talking about, you nutter?' Kim says, quieter now, from the other side of the door. 'Bobbi, you're freaking me out – let me in and give us Jade.'

Now she moves away and she's talking on her phone again but I can only hear snippets.

'Stupid cunt . . . get over here and sort it out!'

Her feet slap slap on the stairs and the downstairs door slams and she is out on the street again, calling Jade's name, shouting up at the window. I get to the part of the story where the horrible little man gets so angry that he stamps his foot and splits himself in two, but Jade doesn't like this bit of the story and she's finished her cream cheese. I take her into the kitchen and give her another one from the fridge.

'Look!' I say. 'The cow's wearing pretty earrings!'

They aren't earrings, they are round packets of cheese hanging from the cow's ears. How can the cow be wearing her own self? The world is in slow motion as I tear off the thin foil wrapping of the cheese and hand it to the girl in my arms, not the farmer's daughter, not my own daughter, someone else's. You bear a daughter and it is almost impossible to bear. I switch on the gas rings, counting them out loud, one, two, three, four, listen to the gas breathing gently then we creep one foot in front of the other, baby steps into the hallway and into the living room where we switch on the television. Loud music, kittens dancing. Jade is mesmerised. I sit her on the sofa, surrounding her with cushions, including the golden unicorn cushion out of her buggy. She watches the dancing kittens. Outside, her mother has grown hysterical and there is another voice now, a neighbour trying to calm her. I move to the window to listen.

'What seems to be the trouble?'

It is Sameer from the shop.

'That fucking paedo is the trouble! I'm meant to be in court – she's going to lose me my kid!'

Through a gap in the curtains I watch Sameer cross the road and knock on Fox's door. He waits outside his house. We are all waiting to see what will happen. Kim scrapes around in the gutter then steps into the middle of the road and lifts her arm. Another stone clatters against the window. In the kitchen, my phone is ringing and on the television kittens prance and dance, their mouths open and shut in time with fairground music.

My phone won't stop ringing so I grab it out of my bag and move swiftly through the flat to chuck it out of the bedroom window. Kim yelps as it smashes on the street below. Andy is there – where did he come from? I duck quickly out of sight. My downstairs neighbours have come out of their flats and are gathered, waiting to see what will happen.

'What about you, you cunt? Get back to Countdown.'

Connor. Bits of my phone case lying in the road and Kim is talking fast, she won't stop talking but I can't hear what she's saying. Sameer has gone back to his shop and is standing in his doorway and now Fox's voice at my door

'Can I come in?' he says, speaking through the letterbox.

I tiptoe into the hallway and I can see his mouth through the slit of the letterbox, his eyes.

'I'm a bit worried, Bobbi . . . say something.'

A loud ticking fills my head, dividing space into before and after. On the television in the other room, kittens are still dancing. The passing of time is torture. I want to smash time, and burn it, see it splintered and broken, spattered across the road, incinerate the seconds, minutes and hours there are left.

Fox's voice outside my door is calm but the words he is saying aren't calm.

'The police are here – they're going to have to force entry.'

There are heavy feet on the stairs and I remember the last time police came to the flat. I run into the living room, to fetch Jade but the gold cushion she is sitting on lifts off the sofa and into the air. I cry out, try to catch it, but it darts out of reach and I chase it into the bedroom where it hovers like a magic carpet next to the open window. Jade doesn't make a sound, but she kicks her little feet to the music coming from the television. Embroidered unicorns, whinnying and snorting, peel themselves off the cushion and lose their golden sheen as they fly out of the window and disappear.

'Don't go!' I shout, as Jade reaches for the unicorns but I can't shut the window in time.

She makes contact with the air and a cry goes up from the pavement below. Jade was in my arms and now she is air. She is dandelion fluff. Outside, people are gathered around something I can't see. I think it might be a squirrel. Kim's mouth is open and she is straining forwards, held around her waist by a female police officer.

Fox appears, escorted out of my building by more police.

'Is it a squirrel?' I call to him out of my open window, but he doesn't answer.

Kim is screaming but sound is delayed, and it's only after a moment that I can hear her and it's as if I've heard that scream before, coming out of my own mouth instead of hers. Then the front door of my flat splits open with a harsh cracking sound and the room is full of strangers.

§

I AM WEARING shoes that aren't mine. These ones squeak on a shiny floor. They remind me of other shoes that squeaked on another shiny floor but I can't remember whose. I think I wrote about the other ones but I don't read what I write, I just write. I write and I am written. I am not a non-person and I am not an outline of a person, but this is a ghost story and I am the ghost. When I finish writing, what is written will be all that's left of me

All that will be left will be marks on a doorframe and these words

No sharp objects allowed, but when someone is with me I can write. I am given a silver pencil that has a propelling lead and a pink rubber at the end.

I am writing a story and soon I'll write the end. It's coming soon, I can feel it.

Here it is.

ACKNOWLEDGEMENTS

THE AUTHOR GRATEFULLY acknowledges assistance from the Authors' Foundation during the writing of this book, and also the loving and practical support in the form of financial loans from the following friends and family: Mum and Dad, Bek and Dom, PV, Julia and Tim Crouch.

Thank you to those who gave me helpful feedback and encouragement on early drafts: Holly Ainley, Peter Boxall, Jac Cattaneo, Julia Crouch, Jane Finigan, Georgia Garrett, Jen Hamilton Emery, Claire Keegan, Candida Lacey, Nina de la Mer, Bethan Roberts, Olga Roberts, Sally O' Reilly, Claire Simpson, Lyn Thomas, Pam Thurschwell, Bosie Vincent, PV, and Meike Ziervogel.

Especial thanks to the families who welcomed me into their lives when I was working as a childminder.

NEW FICTION FROM SALT

RON BUTLIN
Billionaires' Banquet (978-1-78463-100-0)

NEIL CAMPBELL
Sky Hooks (978-1-78463-037-9)

SUE GEE
Trio (978-1-78463-061-4)

CHRISTINA JAMES
Rooted in Dishonour (978-1-78463-089-8)

V.H. LESLIE
Bodies of Water (978-1-78463-071-3)

WYL MENMUIR
The Many (978-1-78463-048-5)

ALISON MOORE
Death and the Seaside (978-1-78463-069-0)

ANNA STOTHARD
The Museum of Cathy (978-1-78463-082-9)

STEPHANIE VICTOIRE
The Other World, It Whispers (978-1-78463-085-0)

ALSO AVAILABLE FROM SALT

ELIZABETH BAINES

Too Many Magpies (978-1-84471-721-7)

The Birth Machine (978-1-907773-02-0)

LESLEY GLAISTER

Little Egypt (978-1-907773-72-3)

ALISON MOORE

The Lighthouse (978-1-907773-17-4)

The Pre-War House and Other Stories (978-1-907773-50-1)

He Wants (978-1-907773-81-5)

Death and the Seaside (978-1-78463-069-0)

ALICE THOMPSON

Justine (978-1-78463-031-7)

The Falconer (978-1-78463-009-6)

The Existential Detective (978-1-78463-011-9)

Burnt Island (978-1-907773-48-8)

The Book Collector (978-1-78463-043-0)

RECENT FICTION FROM SALT

KERRY HADLEY-PRYCE
The Black Country (978-1-78463-034-8)

CHRISTINA JAMES
The Crossing (978-1-78463-041-6)

IAN PARKINSON
The Beginning of the End (978-1-78463-026-3)

CHRISTOPHER PRENDERGAST
Septembers (978-1-907773-78-5)

MATTHEW PRITCHARD
Broken Arrow (978-1-78463-040-9)

JONATHAN TAYLOR
Melissa (978-1-78463-035-5)

GUY WARE
The Fat of Fed Beasts (978-1-78463-024-9)

NEW BOOKS FROM SALT

XAN BROOKS
The Clocks in This House All Tell Different Times
(978-1-78463-093-5)

RON BUTLIN
Billionaires' Banquet (978-1-78463-100-0)

MICKEY J C ORRIGAN
Project XX (978-1-78463-097-3)

MARIE GAMESON
The Giddy Career of Mr Gadd (deceased)
(978-1-78463-118-5)

LESLEY GLAISTER
The Squeeze (978-1-78463-116-1)

NAOMI HAMILL
How To Be a Kosovan Bride (978-1-78463-095-9)

CHRISTINA JAMES
Fair of Face (978-1-78463-108-6)

This book has been typeset by
SALT PUBLISHING LIMITED
using Neacademia, a font designed by Sergei Egorov
for the Rosetta Type Foundry in the Czech Republic.
It is manufactured using Creamy 70gsm, a Forest
Stewardship Council™ certified paper from Stora Enso's
Anjala Mill in Finland. It was printed and bound by
Clays Limited in Bungay, Suffolk, Great Britain.

LONDON
GREAT BRITAIN
MMXVIII